the
mind
is
a
razorblade

max
booth
iii

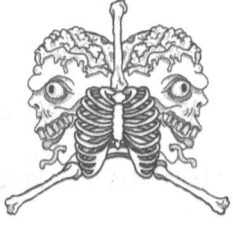

Ghoulish Books
San Antonio, Texas

The Mind is a Razorblade
Copyright © 2024 Max Booth III
First Edition 2014

Second Edition

ISBN: 978-1-943720-80-4

www.Ghoulish.rip

Cover by Betty Rocksteady

also by max booth iii

for lori

i.

familiar strangers

chapter one

Fuck.

Drowning. Choking. Everything is wet, so wet. The water, my lungs—breathe, goddammit, just fucking breathe. *Can't.* Water. So much water. I'm drowning, falling, dying. Cold, so cold. Dark. Breathe.

Can't ...

No. I can.

I must.

Breathe!

I'm coughing and rolling over, but everything is slippery, nothing is tangible. My skin's crusty and ancient. Everything's cold. Even my teeth. A sharp gagging sound emits from my throat and my mouth releases liquids. All other noise becomes muffled. The pain is incredible. A white light explodes within me. Projectile splashes beside me. Face wet, body drenched, I curl up, knees to jaw, hands to shoulders—shaking.

Breathing.

Screaming.

The cries die quickly. Gagging again, drowning and spitting up damnation.

The mud's caked into my mouth and it tastes gritty and bitter. I vomit it all away only to swallow another chunk. Outside in the wet and the cold and I'm drowning, dying, dissipating.

This ground, this earth, I know it. My eyes open slowly, stinging at the mud and the rain infiltrating my vision.

There above, the sky, the darkness. The clouds, the lightning. They're not welcomed. They're the cause of rain, cause of drowning—*death makers*.

Move, must move. Tired, but too cold to sleep. I'm dying. Gotta stay awake. Head's pounding. Fuck. I can't handle this. Everything's exploding. Teeth grind against flesh, digging into my tongue. Mud and rainwater drown my lungs and I try to scream but no sound comes out.

What is this?

And it hits me.

Life. This is life. I am living. Awake. Awake and in pain. But pain is proof I am living. Proof I am awake. This is a good thing. I want to be awake. Awake, but out of this place. Somewhere dry and warm.

Home. I want to be home.

A word, a mystery. It lacks a concrete definition, yet I understand all the same. It is clear. Home is safe. I want to be safe. Safe equals survival, and survival is the ultimate goal. It is the purpose of everything.

I move and goddamn does it hurt. Bones crack, limbs rusted from immobility. I have to take this slow and easy. Patience is essential. I roll over on my stomach, my face pressed against the mud. My flaccid cock digs into the earth and it's so warm, I never want to leave. Vision's blurry, burning, and I close my eyes, unable to continue. Too weak. So damn thirsty my throat's itchy.

Palm flat and fingers arched, nails digging in the mud, I bend my elbows and apply pressure, gaining small levitation before collapsing back in the filth. The water splashes beneath me. Failure.

Second attempt, same results.

Third attempt, success.

Slowly, I'm climbing and rising from my knees, over this fence made of air. I know air. Air is the key to survival. I like air. Now come on. Slow. Steady. Breathe. *Breathe.*

I straighten my back and there's a rough crunching in my spine, followed by exotic pain that quickly subsides. I

4

look up at the sky. The clouds have multiplied. Eyes open, mouth open, the rain penetrates my lungs, washing the mud away.

The pain intensifies with each movement. I grasp my skull and scream. My sore throat worsens when straining my vocal cords, but I can't calm down. The pain is too much. I need help. *Fuck.* Oh god.

God?

Another word I can't comprehend. But I know it. It makes sense. What else? Fuck, I can't. Every time I try to concentrate, another cluster of pain. I do not like pain. Pain is bad. Pain is connected to death. I do not like death.

I do not *want* death.

But death wants me.

Something's moving in my chest. My heart. It's beating so fast, so fast. I'm convinced it's going to abandon me in the mud. But this heart, it's mine. It's the source of power, the source of life.

I have to relax, have to gather my thoughts. *Think.* It is night. It is raining. I am in pain. I am cold.

I am afraid.

I close my eyes and inhale, allowing a few moments to pass before exhaling. I do this awhile, awaiting my life force to return to normality. The rain only aggravates, makes it too cold. I need warmth, safety.

I open my eyes and slowly take in my surroundings. Everything is dark and wet. Breathing slow, my heartbeat relaxes. Slow, I think, you gotta go slow.

Slowly but surely, sugar pie.

Words that aren't my own, but in my head nonetheless. Words I know, but cannot grasp. Words familiar with home. Words that provide warmth.

Whatever they are, they seem to work. The environment around me fades into focus. I am born into the here and now.

I am here. I am now.

I am awake.

I look down and discover a pair of feet connected to a pair of legs, connected to a body, connected to a head protecting a mind which throbs and pulsates like a monster breaking from its chains. My feet are encased with a thick layer of mud created by the rain, attacking the earth, molesting the grass. Not green but black. It flows beneath me, down a slope and toward a nearby stream of water.

River.

But the rain is too persistent, too heavy. It causes the river to flood upon the land. Fuck my head. My skull pounds like the rain pounds against the earth.

There's a set of lights off in the distance and somehow I know they're from the headlights of an automobile. A vehicle. A car. Everybody knows cars. *I* know cars.

The rain blurs the lights, making it almost nonexistent. It's enough to aid my eyes, enough to see I'm not the only one abandoned in the mud, in the madness.

Between me and the car I spot a large shape on the ground, hidden in the darkness. Almost shadow-like, but clearly a solid object.

I crouch down and there's another painful crunch in my legs. I dig one unstable palm into the ground to maintain balance. The other hand creeps out and touches the body. I grab its shoulder and turn it around on its back.

A man, like me.

He does not breathe like I breathe.

His eyes are open but caked with mud. Same goes for his mouth. Somehow I know to check his neck and wrist for a pulse. I feel nothing.

He is dead. Here, but not.

I am afraid.

He's wearing a black trench coat, with other clothing underneath. I lean down for a closer inspection and discover rips in the fabric. Small circular holes here and there along his chest. This man has been shot. More than once, too. Someone made this man dead.

Soul takers.

Did I do this?

If so, why?

My body shakes, my teeth chatter. The rain. The night air. I am going to freeze to death, become nonexistent like the man beside me. The man with the large, warm coat.

Where did my clothes go? Surely I didn't come here naked. Someone must have taken them. Taken them along with the rest of my identity.

I flip him back on his stomach and pull off the coat, standing up and slipping my arms through the sleeves. It ends a little past my knees. I button it up with haste, enjoying the desired warmth it delivers.

I step over the corpse and my foot lands on something hard in the ground. Something else cold, something steel.

I pick up the mysterious object, bringing it closer to my face. The weight feels natural in my hand.

It is a gun.

A big gun, too. Silver. Heavy, but not uncomfortably heavy—*reassuringly heavy*. Yes, a gun. I know guns.

But do I like them?

I hold onto it for safekeeping and drop it in the lower right-side pocket of my new coat. The weight sags it down, making me feel uneven.

I continue my short journey to the car up ahead, and as I gain distance I discover this is no ordinary vehicle. White, with paint on the sides, glass bulbs attached to the top. I know this type of car.

This is a cop car.

I know cops, too. Cops are the law, and the law helps ensure survival.

At least, they're supposed to.

The driver's door is wide open. I walk around the side and find another man on his back in the mud, this one wearing a much smaller coat. When I turn him over, the tie around his neck begins blowing wildly with the wind. A crusted star is pinned to his belt. It stares at me, judging.

He has just as many bullet holes in him as the other man.

Only, unlike the other man, this one is coughing.

Like me, he is alive.

I smile at him, relieved to not be the only one still breathing in this fucked-up flood. The rain is so heavy I can barely make out his face. I lean forward and the whites of his eyes widen in the darkness.

I try to speak, but my throat's too raw to produce anything coherent.

"No!" he shouts at me, and his hand fumbles in the interior of his jacket. It occurs to me that this cop is here for a reason, and odds are it has something to do with me. Who's to say I wasn't the one to shoot him originally?

Speaking of shooting, what the hell is he reaching for?

Shit.

No time to think.

Act.

Before you can't.

I reach into my pocket and grab the gun, quickly aiming the barrel through the fabric of the trench coat and squeezing the trigger. The rain is loud, but not as loud as the gunshot. The cop's face darkens in the shadows and his body goes limp.

I'm disappointed that I'm not more surprised at my instincts. I've done this before. I feel it. Shooting people is not a new thing.

A sudden crackling from inside the car nearly sends me to the ground. Somehow I manage to calm my nerves and step over the man I just shot. I sit down in the driver's seat and stare at the radio blowing up with static.

"Unit 84, this is dispatch. Do you read?"

I sit there, frozen.

"Officer Oasis, do you read? Copy, do you read? Units are en route to GPS's location. Do you read? Unit 84?"

I raise the mic to my mouth, forgetting how to breathe

again. All I have to do is click the button and the machine will hear me. So why is it so difficult?

"Unit 84, units are en route. Backup is on the way. I repeat, Unit 84, backup is on the way. Hang in there, Officer. Help is coming."

My thumb presses down on the button and I am free to say whatever I please. Oxygen weighing down like an anchor, it's a struggle to enunciate.

"H-he-hello?"

The reply is nearly simultaneous.

"Unit 84, is that you? Officer Oasis? Do you read me? Hello? What is your status? Unit 84, do you read me?"

No. I think. I am not Officer Oasis. Officer Oasis is dead. Dead by my hand. I, on the other hand, am alive. Alive and in serious trouble.

"Unit 84, is that you? Officer Oasis? Do you read me?"

I drop the mic and climb out of the car, emerging back into the rain. Into my womb. It's a miracle I don't fall straight on my face. Somehow I manage to push my legs against the earth and run.

As the rain pushes me deeper into the woods, I hear the distant wails of sirens approaching.

I do not look back.

chapter two

And I continue not looking back until I can no longer move. My body takes a shallow dive into a dirty puddle and my knees sigh in relief. The rain isn't as loud now, but the weather is colder. With the rain fading, the wind picks up. Makes me shiver, makes me ache. It helps to keep moving. Nothing can get me as long as I don't stop.

But of course I've stopped.

Those sirens I hear aren't in my head. They are very much real—and gaining, by the sound of it.

Teeth sink into my tongue as another wave of pain implodes. First chance I get, I'll need to examine my head more closely. But right now I have greater concerns. Such as getting the fuck out of the cold and finding shelter.

Such as remembering my name.

I grasp onto a moldy tree stump and pull myself up. Breathing heavy, I push forward, my chest on fire. I don't know where I'm going and I don't know what I'll do when I get there. All I know is as long as I keep moving, nothing can touch me.

I am unstoppable.

Then I trip over a fallen tree branch and fly face first into the dirt, head banging against a rock.

The migraine multiples by infinity, an echo of agony reverberating throughout my skull. I scream and punch the ground. My toes throb and suddenly I regret passing up on the chance to steal the dead man's shoes back at the river.

So maybe I'm not that unstoppable after all.

I gag and spit out a mouthful of mud and struggle back to my feet. Using decomposing roots as leverage, I boost myself up a steep hill seemingly crafted entirely of sludge.

How long had it been raining before I woke up?

Has it always rained?

Will it ever stop?

When I finally reach the top of the hill, ten seconds pass before I misstep and tumble down the other side. I reach blindly for roots and trees, anything sturdy enough to brace the inevitable fall, but come up empty. My body rolls too fast, intoxicating all my senses with a gust of ultimate turbulence. There is no choice but to allow destiny to work its magic.

And evidently destiny's magic involves a confused man in a trench coat rolling off the base of a muddy hill and freefalling through the air, bouncing off the lid of a dumpster and landing with a thud against solid concrete.

For a moment, I am convinced every bone in my body breaks at once.

My back arches and twists, and my eyes bulge from their sockets as all the wind within me escapes in a storm I can't prevent. My mouth unhinges like a tarnished screen door being forced open. My vision spins and spirals and a piercing bell rings inside my skull.

I can't feel my legs at first, and I fear I've been paralyzed. Maybe I will die here like I should have died at the river. Maybe I'm already dead. Then the pain hits my legs, hits my entire body, and everything is white noise.

Minutes, hours, days pass with me beside the dumpster writhing and gasping.

After a while, I manage to sit up. I'll still live.

I hope.

There is some comfort in finally escaping the woods. This new area is considerably more expansive than my previous surroundings, and it helps the rain is mostly down to a light drizzle. I'm in a small rectangle of pavement, the dumpster resting at the end of the area. A narrow path of concrete built over a large flatland of wet grass leads from here to an unknown spot up ahead, meandering around trees and bushes.

The correct label for this setting is right on the tip of my tongue, yet I can't quite place it. I know it. Goddammit, *I know it,* so what is it?

It's a . . . it's . . . oh, fuck it. This is just pathetic. I don't need to know the name. The name won't help me with what I need. Just more useless knowledge to interrupt my progress.

I follow the trail into the night, dripping from head to toe. With the rain all but nonexistent now, the petrichor from the slowly drying grass seeps into my nostrils and soothes my senses. It's a dusty scent, a feeling of calmness.

Every dozen or so paces I come across a small, steel mesh wastebasket along the side of the trail with short lampposts sticking in the ground beside them. All of the cans are overflowing with garbage. Most of the bulbs are long dead. Who comes here?

Here . . .

This inability to come up with a name is more painful than anything I've experienced thus far. More painful than my head—whatever's wrong with my head. More painful than the free-fall I did onto a dumpster. Okay, maybe not that painful.

I stop and refuse to budge another inch until whoever's in charge of this particular torture session decides to let me have just this one.

Tell me. What the hell is the word? Think, man, just think. You know this. It's so simple. As soon as you remember you're going to feel like the world's biggest idiot.

I close my eyes tight and strain my brain in concentration. It pains my head to think so hard but I'm too goddamn stubborn to let it go. *Think, just fucking think—*

The glass bulb from one of the lampposts next to me explodes.

I crouch down, snapping my head around in every direction, searching for a perpetrator of the bulb explosion. But there's no one else here, at least not that I can see.

I am all alone.

And just like that, a word leaves my lips, almost as if someone else has taken control of my mouth:

"Park."

But I no longer give a shit about knowing the word. All I'm thinking about is the bulb that exploded for no reason at all. The bulb that exploded when my brain was a strain away from having an aneurysm.

Shit.

Up ahead at one of the few lamps still burning light, I find a bench accompanying its small illuminated territory. I recline on the wooden boards, allowing its cruel toughness to press against my spine.

I stare at another bulb and concentrate, thinking *blow up,* thinking *shatter,* thinking *explode.*

Thinking *mind powers.*

Thinking *psychokinesis.*

Thinking *oh shit.*

But the bulb remains the same. Nothing happens.

The other light could have blown for any number of reasons. Calm down. I didn't do it. That's crazy.

Next to me, written on the bench in bright neon green spray paint, is the word: *CONUNDRAE.*

The word leaves a metallic taste in my mouth.

Sitting under the lamp's gloomy projections, I wonder why it is that I can have so much trouble remembering the word "park" when other words like "lamp" and "bench" come naturally. Maybe because I hadn't *tried* to name the bench and lamp. The words were just there, waiting to be picked up by my whirlwind of oblivion as I passed. But "park", on the other hand, hadn't been in the same vicinity, forcing me to actually stop and think about it. And that pause, that forced act of concentration, had been my mistake. It's the same reason I can't remember my name, or any other shred of identity. I'm thinking about it too hard. Maybe if I just sit back, relax, it will all naturally fade back into focus. I mean, it's not like this condition is going to last forever.

Right?

I gulp, fearing the cold silence. My toes curl up against the bottoms of my feet. The night seems to drop at least three degrees every five minutes. I slide my hands in my coat pockets in a feeble search for warmth and touch the cold steel of the gun hidden inside. It's amazing it hadn't gotten lost during my tumble down the hill. Another miracle that it hadn't gone off and shot me in the balls.

I'd shot someone. Hadn't even hesitated.

Of course, the cop had been reaching for his own gun. I can't let myself forget it'd been self-defense. I'm not a killer. I'm just a survivor.

Repeat it, goddammit.

I'm not a killer.

I'm not a killer.

I'm not a killer.

I'm . . . I don't know what I am.

It's pathetic. I was given a name. I wasn't born a nobody. Someone named me. Someone thought I was important enough to have my very own unique title, just for myself and no one else.

And somehow I've lost that title.

My parents must be so ashamed. If they're even alive. I know about parents. I don't know what they look like but I know I've had a pair at least once in my life. They could very well be as dead as the two men back at the river. But if they're alive, are they looking for me? Are they worried? Is *anyone* looking for me?

Should they be worried?

Sitting on the bench, fingers caressing the steel of the gun, I think I'd have to say yes, they should be worried.

I sure as hell am.

My free hand slides into the opposite pocket of the

trench coat and comes up with a tiny cardboard box housing half a dozen wet matches. On the back of the matchbox there's a cartoon of a busty pinup girl. The words THE RISQUÉ CABARET are stamped around her in red font.

The corpse back at the river must have visited this place recently. Maybe I've been there, too. Maybe I can find some answers there, someone who knows me. Some peace of mind.

Now I just have to find it.

I return the matchbook and search the rest of the coat. The only other item I find is hiding in the left inside pocket: a medium sized plastic chip. It's painted a darkish blue, and the word "indigo" comes to mind. That's what this shade of blue is called. Indigo. But there's something else about this word, something much bigger than just the color . . .

Of course I have no idea. Just a feeling. A real bad feeling.

There's a number painted on both sides of the chip: $2000.

My rest here has expired. By now, the police have undoubtedly discovered the bodies at the river, and I am not yet ready for them to catch me. There's other business to take care of before that can happen.

Such as finding this Risqué Cabaret.

Wherever this place is, there are answers. There is closure. I am sure of it.

Well, okay, I'm a *little* sure.

chapter three

The rest of the park is much of the same. At the end there's more trees. I dig my feet into puddles of mud and slop and follow the darkness. I don't know where I'm going, but anywhere besides the river will be a considerable improvement. Soon the mud is replaced by the hard concrete of a walking trail, leading out of the woods again and into some sort of alley.

I've found the city.

The buildings grow taller the farther away they stand. Ancient wooden boards are nailed across doors and windows. Maybe one of every four buildings is still in use. There are no vehicles in sight.

I've been here before.

I'm not so sure I like this place.

A sea of wet, hot garbage infiltrates my senses. The sound of people erupts from the end of the alley. I hurry forward, stepping onto a sidewalk, abandoning my isolation.

Massive crowds swarm the streets in either direction. The thought of moving forward terrifies me. Instead I back away, consumed by claustrophobia, until a streetlamp bounces me back toward the street. There's no escaping this.

I try to count how many people are here but it's a lunatic's game. Hundreds. Maybe thousands. Some don't talk, others yell as loud as their lungs will allow. An unnerving herd of pedestrians pushing themselves forward, heading left, heading right, heading somewhere, heading nowhere.

The silent ones possess no expressions upon their faces. It's like they don't even realize they're awake. Like they don't exist. Robots flipped to autopilot. Some push rusted shopping carts, stopping every once in a while to throw in a random piece of junk they seem to consider valuable. Others bump into streetlamps over and over, refusing to try a different direction. Either they're too stupid to step aside or they simply don't care, and I don't know which option is more alarming.

But not all of them are so dead inside. Others run back and forth, screaming, shouting, crying. Some punch the walls until their fists are obliterated and drive their heads through random glass windows.

"Are you blind?" they scream.

"We will all pay!"

"Conundrae is coming!"

Many of these lunatics carry cardboard signs with phrases like "CONUNDRAE WILL RISE!" and "WE ARE FUCKED!" scribbled across them.

All of them wear dirty rags. Streaks of dirt smear their faces. Hair crusty and eyes grey, all infected with a universal disease known to everyone except for me. Where are they going? What are they thinking? What do they know that I don't?

Apparently everything.

Conundrae.

An image of teeth grinding against teeth. The sound of blood dripping upon concrete. The taste of flesh tearing from bone.

Conundrae. Conundrae.

What are you, Conundrae?

And why does it hurt so much to think about you?

The sudden roar of a monorail snaps my attention, reminding me the world doesn't take a time-out every time some asshole loses his memory and experiences an existential crisis. My teeth chatter in unison with the monorail rattling against the aerial tracks above us all, shaking my skin and blurring my vision.

In a daze, I step forward and plunge into the masses. Wherever all these people are going, maybe it's somewhere I also belong. They could all have the right idea. Maybe salvation lies just at the end of the road.

Only thing is, there's two ways to go for every road.

Which do I choose?

One way could lead to all the answers, and the other could lead to absolutely nothing.

Both ways could have answers.

Both ways could end with brick walls, too.

I briefly entertain the idea of shooting myself in the head, letting all uncertainties and anguish pour out through the Bullet Hole of Relief, but I can't seem to find the strength to reach in my pocket, so I forget the idea.

A nude passerby sporting long feathers clipped to his hair stands out among the crowd. The massive piercing dangling from his genitalia makes him seem especially interesting, so without another moment's thought I start following him.

"Hey!" I shout, jogging through the crowd and wincing when my bare feet connect with a rough patch of gravel. I grab his shoulder and pull him toward me, saying, "Hey, guy, wait a minute, I need your help."

The naked man pushes my hand off his shoulder and steps back.

"Wait," I say, "don't go. I just need some help. I'm trying to find a place called The Risqué Cabaret. Do you know it?"

He shakes his head and drops to his knees. His eyes tear up and he clenches his hands together underneath his chin, praying.

A single word leaves his mouth, over and over, in one continuous chant loud enough to be heard over the rest of the vagrants.

"Conundrae, Conundrae, Conundrae, Conundrae, Conundrae, Conundrae."

"What the fuck does that *mean?*" I scream at him, and my voice only makes him cry louder.

"CO. NUN. DRAE. CO. NUN. DRAE. CO. NUN. DRAE."

This man is crazier than I am.

I step aside and continue deeper into the city. I sidestep small mountains of rubble, frequently bumping into others. Even then their monotonous expressions do not falter.

I know these people, but I cannot remember them, and it is the saddest thing in the world.

I want to apologize to these familiar strangers.

I want to hug them and make them tell me everything is going to be all right.

But they would only be lying, and I would know the truth.

A man and a woman hold each other as they stand together on the sidewalk, leaning against a wall. When I get closer, I realize they're asleep. The man balances the woman and the woman balances the man. Together they keep each other from falling.

If I woke them up, would they babble nonsense like everyone else?

No, I could never disturb them. Let them sleep for a thousand years and never reawake to this nightmare. It is my gift to them.

Maybe I have someone waiting for me, too. Someone for me to lean against. Somebody who's worried about me. Parents? If not them, then who? I try to think but it only sharpens the migraine.

Hell, I don't even know how old I am—never mind if I'm sleeping with somebody. Guessing my birthdate is also a waste of time, but the word "Pisces" suddenly jumps out at me just as I give up trying, and a brief image flashes before my eyes, conjuring up an oil painting of two purple fish bound together by their mouths with a short string of silver. I remember *(remember?)* the painting hanging there above the table at that Greek restaurant, and how I'd tried to imagine what life would be like tied to another's mouth, caught in some kind of demented kiss lasting all of eternity.

Greek restaurant?

The vision hits me hard, and my legs give out. Waves of imagery wash through me and I am lost.

Lost in a painting . . .

(i am sitting in a bright orange booth, elbows resting on the table, fingers tapping the back of the menu in my hands as i pretend to scan the listed contents. the pisces painting hangs on the wall directly to my right. i can't describe the mood it sets, but it's perfect. so perfect. a woman sits across from me, another menu in her hands. i see hair. red hair. beautiful red hair. so red it's intoxicating. so intriguing i can't remember how to think. and those eyes, those marvelous green eyes—enthralling. everything begins to shake and pixelate, the redhead's face dissolving into a grainy partition of oblivion, and the restaurant implodes, turning everything into nothing.)

My body continues shaking in the city streets. I manage to crawl away before anyone steps on me, sitting up against a wall and taking a breather. I close my eyes and try to return to the restaurant, but it's no use. The girl is gone, and already I miss her so much it hurts.

"What the fuck are you doing there on the ground, man?" shouts a man above me.

I nearly scream. I snap my head up and give him my full attention, fearing he's about to attack. He waits on the sidewalk nearby, holding a half-smoked cigarette. His bald head glistens under the muted glow of a streetlight. He wears a dark blue button-up shirt, collars pointing straight up.

Indigo, the color is indigo . . .

"Excuse me?" I mumble, suddenly afraid the man might be a hallucination.

"I said, what the fuck is your problem? You're gonna get trampled. You of all people should fuckin' know better."

I clear my throat, frantically climbing to my feet to meet him at eye-level. "You . . . you *know* me?"

"What?"

"What do you mean, 'you of all people'?"

"Shit, man, you know what I mean. You travel these streets more than anyone else."

"No." I edge closer to him. "Please tell me."

The man raises his brow, looking at me like I'm a lunatic, and he's right.

"Uh, I need to get back inside," he says, and turns around toward a set of doors a block down. The doors project a bright light from inside the building, and I don't understand how I'm only just now noticing them.

"You're late—you know that, right?" he says over his shoulder. "Lamb is gonna be seriously pissed, man."

I have to shield my eyes as I step through the automatic sliding doors. The light is harsh and violent. My eyes go into overtime attempting to adjust. The waxed floor squeaks beneath my feet. The bald man walks behind the counter and I meet him on the opposite side, a cash register and a bin of condoms between us. Racks of cigarette cartons are inserted into the wall behind him— which are fifty percent off, according to the banner stretched above them.

"What the hell are you wearing?" The clerk nods at my getup.

"A coat."

"No shit."

There's something about this man, now that I've had a chance to see him in full light. I'm not sure what it is exactly, but I know I do not like him.

I don't think he likes me, either.

"The fuck are you looking at me like that for?"

"Huh?"

"Stop staring at me like that," the clerk says. "You're creeping me out."

"We don't like each other too much, do we?"

The clerk eyes me funny, pressing his hands on the counter and leaning forward. "You fuckin' with me?"

"I'm not sure," I say, and I'm telling the truth. "Look, why don't you just tell me what my name is? Then we can move on from there."

The clerk sneers. "Where in the hell have you been, anyway?"

"I don't know."

"Whatever. I don't care. Just make sure Lamb knows this has nothing to do with me. It's late because of *you*. Got it?"

"*What?*"

I jump back as the clerk pounds his fist on the counter. "Listen here, asshole, quit screwing around for once and do what you're paid to do. *Both* of our jobs are at stake here. *Comprende*, retard?"

"Um."

He sighs and bends under the counter, coming back up with a hefty shoulder bag. He drops it on the clear surface of the counter between us.

"There ya go, smartass. Now get the hell out of my store."

"First tell me my name."

"Fuck off."

"At least tell me *something*."

"Okay, how about you're really beginning to piss me off?"

"Fair enough. What about some food?"

"What?"

"Food. I want some food. And something for my head. It's killing me."

He sighs again. "You serious?"

I nod.

"Hell, man, you wanna take a shower in my employees' bathroom while you're at it? You disgusting little fuck—look at you!" He pauses and rubs his temple, then points back at the end of the store. "Goddammit, just hurry up."

I do not need to be told twice. I turn around and head where he's directed me, jogging down an aisle searching for something that looks good enough to eat. My stomach would settle for about anything right now.

I grab a pastry and tear the wrapper in half with my teeth, devouring the contents within seconds. I take a chocolate bar and stuff it in my coat pocket for later. Two aisles down I choose a nice big bottle of ibuprofen, take four of them and slip the bottle in with the chocolate bar. Next I make my way over to the cooler section and take out a can of beer, gulping it all down in one desperate motion.

I manage a weak smile at the progress my mind seems to be making. An hour ago I don't think I would have even been able to comprehend what a can of beer was, never mind ibuprofen.

Slowly but surely, sugar pie . . .

There's that voice again. It's the second time I've heard it now. It isn't my own, but still, the voice is comforting. Almost motherly.

Hell, who knows, it probably is my mother's voice. It makes sense. But where the hell is she, then? All I have of her is one little phrase. A phrase she must have used all the time, apparently, otherwise I doubt I'd be hearing it now, in these most ugly of times.

"Hey, man, what the fuck are you doing back there?"

"Coming . . . "

I hurry back to the front of the store. The clerk is how I left him—arms crossed, one hell of an annoyed look across his face.

He could be planning a way to kill me. I don't know what this man is capable of doing. Truth is, I don't even know what *I'm* capable of doing, never mind somebody else. We could all be coldblooded killers.

"Took you long enough," the clerk says, intensifying his glare.

"Thanks."

"Shut up."

"Tell me my name."

"I am going to beat the shit out of you."

"Funny enough," I say, cracking a smile, "I was just thinking you wouldn't mind doing just that."

The clerk returns the smile. "Glad to hear we're on the same terms then. Now leave."

I nod in agreement and head toward the front doors.

"Um, don't you think you're forgetting something?"

I stop and slowly turn around, facing the clerk again. Then I see the shoulder bag on the counter.

"Oh, yeah."

I walk back over and start to unzip the bag, but he pushes my hands away. "Are you *crazy?* Don't fucking open that. You'll be lucky if it hasn't spoiled as it is."

"Oh, okay, sorry." I throw the strap over my shoulder and heave it up off the counter. It's a lot heavier than anticipated, and I have to put up a fight not to double over with it. "So, um, where was it that I'm supposed to take this again?"

The clerk answers me with a cold stare and refuses to say anything else. I take it as my cue to leave, lest he decides to fulfill his dreams of breaking my face.

I stop outside the drugstore, loitering under one of the few streetlights that still seem to be functioning. I crouch down and find a seat atop the curb, relishing in the weight it relieves. I breathe in the night air, glad that I've left the bright store and returned to my dark sanctum.

The city vagrants step on my bare toes as they pass, and I shout and curse at them, but they don't seem to hear me.

I unzip the bag to reveal a large orange box with a white lid. A cooler. You put ice in these. Things you want to keep cold. Beer, soda, hamburger . . . other things . . .

Bad things.

Opening this bag suddenly feels like a horrible idea. Maybe I should leave it here on the sidewalk and get as far away from the thing as possible.

While you still can, an ominous voice in my head adds.

"Shut up, ominous voice," I mutter under my breath.

I pop open the lid and look down, face wincing overdramatically in preparation for Hell itself to spring out at me.

But all I see is ice.

And the top of a very large re-sealable zipper bag.

Hesitant, I pull the bag out of the cooler, feeling the cold ridges of more ice inside. I unzip the top and discover another bag inside this one. Only there is no ice inside this second bag. No, no ice at all.

Instead, it is half filled with a dark reddish liquid.

Blood.

And the rest of the contents . . .

I may have only been born a few hours ago in a river of mud, but I'll be damned if I don't know what it is that I'm looking at. I try to look away but I can't. For the first time tonight I find myself wishing my memory is worse off than it already is.

I don't want to know about this.

I don't want any part of this.

I don't want to understand what I'm staring at is called a heart—a precious life force that once belonged to another human being.

Once belonged.

Now this heart belongs to no one. Its previous host has fallen victim to the nevermore. Now it is in my hands. My *hands.* Oh god, why . . . ?

I can't hold back the scream from my lungs as I fling the bag off my lap. It thuds against the road and rolls a few feet to a complete stop. Only a couple seconds pass before a man in dirty underwear scoops it up, giving the heart a quick onceover and tossing it in his shopping cart like such discoveries are perfectly normal.

I squeal and kick hard against the concrete, frantically pedaling backward using my hands, quickly running out of room and smacking against the brick wall of the drugstore's exterior. Eyes bulging out of their sockets, I attempt a continuation of my backpedaling, only to smash my skull against hard concrete once more. A part of me realizes what I'm doing, but a much larger part of me doesn't care. There are more important matters to deal with at the moment than to worry about some silly little headache.

Such as the whole "holy shit that was a fucking heart" aspect running all sense of coherency into total pandemonium.

chapter four

Because holy shit, that was a fucking heart.

Breathe. *Breathe.* Crap, crap, crap. *Breathe.* Don't you dare panic. Calm *down.* But I can't. I can't do anything besides focus on the fact that I've just thrown a human heart across the road with my own bare hands.

Despite the memory loss, it still seems like I shouldn't be too freaked out by this. Obviously this is the way of life, and I must have gotten used to it at some point in time—right?

So why can't I now?

Shouldn't the acceptance come as naturally as any other action I've done tonight? Like, say, steal a gun from a dead body, or shoot a cop?

I shake my head, disgusted.

No, this isn't the same. This is different.

This is a human fucking heart. I have one just like it, only mine is still pumping blood. Whereas this other heart is traveling by way of shopping cart.

Jesus Christ, what *is* this?

I don't want to know, but I do. This is life. Everyone else can accept this but myself. Something must have happened to reprogram my mind, tamper with the wires within my brain to turn me into some kind of oblivious Neanderthal.

Neanderthal?

I know what a Neanderthal is but I still can't comprehend the thought of holding someone's heart in my hands. Still can't remember my own name. Still can't find my way home.

Home.

That's where I need to be. Home. Safety and warmth. Before it's too late.

The weight of the gun in my pocket is suddenly all too aware of itself.

I stand up. Turn around. Head back into the store. The doors close behind me. The piercing scream of light bleeds into my eyes.

I stride toward the checkout counter. The clerk sits on a stool, reading a magazine with a woman spreading her legs on the cover. Despite the large population of vagrants passing by outside, we are still the only two in the store.

The clerk sets down his magazine, opens his mouth to say something, something that I doubt will answer any of my questions. Something I don't want to hear. I pull out the gun from my trench coat, swing my arm sideways, and hear the destructive crack of the gun's butt colliding into his cheekbone, smashing into his teeth. A glob of something red and menacing flings from his mouth and splatters against the cash register.

He goes down.

I don't allow him any time to put up a defense. Scrambling over the counter, I leap on top of him. He gasps and I clock him again with the gun.

I bring my face close to his, my teeth gritted together, trying my best not to tear them into his throat and drink his blood.

"What the fuck is going on?" I scream.

He gives me an answer I do not like, an answer that does not help me. I grab him by his neck and begin pounding his skull against the floor in unison with each syllable I spit out: "What. The. Fuck. Is. Go. Ing. On."

I'm a starving animal finally gone wild.

This is my feast.

"Tell me."

28

"Tell you *what?*" the clerk cries, locked in my gaze.

"Why was there a heart in that bag?"

"*What?*"

I repeat my question with another thwack of the gun. Teeth shatter and he chokes on his own blood.

"C-c-conun-un-drae," he stammers. "Sh-shit, m-man, same reason we do any of this. Have you lost your lo-love? Your loy-loyalty?"

"Conundrae?"

The clerk spits out a chunk of blood. "Goddamn, dude, did you have some bad sh-shrooms or something?"

I clear my throat and calm my tone. "What is my name?"

And he laughs.

He *laughs.*

"Oh my god," the clerk says, "you really have lost it, haven't you?"

He laughs again. Laughing like *he's* the one who's lost it, and not me. Laughing like he knows he's right. Maybe he is. Either way, it's just what my animal urges need to trigger blindness upon all I possess that was once rational.

I snap.

The pain in my head increases to the point where it doesn't even hurt. Eyes water, nose exhales air, lungs strangle themselves as they attempt to pump oxygen, ears feeling like they're on fire. I can no longer think. My heart pounds furiously against my chest, almost as if it is trying to escape, trying to join the other heart in the shopping cart. The one belonging to some corpse that's probably a lot better off than I am.

I snap not like a tree branch, but a bone.

I picture bashing my fists into his face until there's nothing left, but before I can move, the clerk suddenly screams loud and miserably, and his eyeballs go from white to red within a second. A stream of blood ejects from his mouth and his skin cracks like desert rock under a cruel sun. The cracks fill up with more blood and I barely have enough time to scramble off his body before his head pops like a balloon. Blood and brain matter splatter against me and a skull fragment cuts my cheek open.

I'm left alone in the drug store, sitting next to this headless corpse, crying and trying my best not to have a heart attack.

His head.

It exploded because of me. *I did that.*

I made his goddamn head explode.

Jesus fucking Christ.

What have I done?

What kind of monster am I?

I sit here a few more minutes, catching my breath, and try to stand back up. It's a struggle not to slip. I hear the electronic *beep-bloop* of the automatic doors sliding open and I spin around, pistol shaking in my hand. I conceal the weapon behind my back, but choose to leave one timid finger curled around the trigger lest more trouble should arise.

A man approaches the front desk. His hairy legs stick out of his loosely-tied fluffy blue robe, his feet protected by a pair of slippers with bunny heads bobbling on top. They make me wish I had some footwear of my own. All I have is blood.

Whistling, he casually points at the cigarette racks behind me and says, "Pack of Pinkly's, in the red. Thanks."

"Um."

I try to act, but I can't. If I could just turn around, grab the cigarettes and take this guy's money before he looks down behind the counter, then maybe I'll be okay. Not to mention that—

"Hey, what the fuck?" the robed man yells, pointing at the corpse beside my feet, backing away against a rack of hats.

Shit.

I clear my throat, the gun behind my back becoming heavier and heavier by the second. "Yes?"

"What . . . what happened to that guy's head?"

"Um."

"Did you do that?"

"Uh."

"You did, didn't you?"

"Well."

He places his hands on his hips and appears to contemplate the situation. "You don't work here then, do you?"

"Not exactly."

I go to scratch the back of my neck to cure my nerves, but in the process of lifting my arm I foolishly reveal the gun in my hand, causing the robed man to jump back against the fancy hat rack all over again.

"Jesus!" he says.

It's a miracle I don't drop the gun.

"Look, all I have is enough for the smokes, I swear." He starts to dig into the pockets of his robe. "Here, take it."

I shake my head. "Keep your money."

This only seems to frighten him more. "What? What do you want then? Are you going to shoot me? Fine, do it! Shoot me! No one else will . . . "

"I . . . I'm not going to shoot you."

His face drops, disappointed. "So you don't want *anything*?"

I consider it for a moment, deciding there *is* something in his possession I could use. Using the gun, I gesture to his feet.

"The slippers, take them off."

"What?"

"I want your slippers."

He glances at his feet and slowly raises his head, dumbfounded. "But . . . but these are my funny bunnies. They are my favorite."

"I don't care. You wanna get shot? Huh?"

"Yes! Please, god, do it! Blow my brains out all over my funny bunnies, Mista Gunman!"

31

I wave the gun at him and scream, "Goddammit, hand over the slippers!"

"Fine!" he cries out, and kicks them off his feet. They go soaring over the counter and bounce off my chest, landing in the puddle of blood on the floor.

"Thank you." I slide my feet into the funny bunnies, reveling in the warmth they provide.

"Comfy?" the robed man asks, juggling balance as he adjusts to the cold temperatures of his bare feet pressing against the linoleum.

"Yes, very." I move around the counter and head for the doors.

"You're leaving, huh? Just like that?"

"Yup."

"Okay." He pauses. "Well, I guess I will just help myself then."

"You do that."

I don't make it ten feet from the drugstore before the others outside catch on to what's happening inside. Glass shatters and people shout in celebration. Shopping carts rattle as they zip through the already broken-down entrance, on their way to empty the shelves of their stock. It occurs to me only now that maybe I should have tried doing the same. Who knows the next time I'll come across a chance for free food.

I don't turn around, not for a second. This is not any of my business. Okay, maybe it is a little bit, considering I was the one who went all freaky head-popper on the clerk—but still, I will have no part in this anarchic aftermath.

Tonight, these city dwellers will have their fun. Their long-awaited moment of glorious looting—all for one, one for all, and all for anyone with quick enough hands. I may not know what exactly is going on here, but what I do know is many starving children will go to bed satisfied tonight, and somehow I can't seem to find the harm in this.

Maybe if I hadn't been dealing with a man whose work

had something to do with stolen hearts, I'd be seeing a different side to this.

So fuck him.

And fuck whoever else is involved in all of this.

Fuck them all.

With everyone's attention directed to the drugstore, this place has turned into a ghost town. Only it's not a ghost town—it's a dark, oblivious metropolis. And I am the only ghost here. Just me, the ghost with the big coat and funny bunny slippers. The ghost without a name.

Despite the crowd's sudden absence, I can still hear them riot in the drugstore. Tribal yells of the young and the restless. Anarchy prevails. I hear them shouting in chaotic glee and it fills me with a sense of uneasiness.

I can't resist and steal a glance over my shoulder. The drugstore, only a hundred feet away or so, is ruined. The windows, the doors—all shattered. Mounds of glass pile up along the walls as sharp little mountains, awaiting the first unlucky bystander to pass by without any shoes. I feel sorry for the robed funny bunny owner. I'd taken his slippers, and for all I know I may have caused him to get an infection on the bottom of his foot. Hell, they may have to resort to amputation. I'm such a bastard.

But the broken glass isn't what fills me with dread. I can see inside the store, and what I see is mesmerizing.

Fire.

Smoke seeps through the windows at the top of the building like a surreptitious soul escaping from its doomed host.

People flee with carts full of material goods, shit-eating grins plastered across their sad, silly faces like they can't believe what's happening, but they've put up with enough to know not to question when a spontaneous glimpse of fortune is blessed upon them from out of nowhere.

They're just going to let it ride, and when the ride comes to an end, at least they'll have a good story to tell those who weren't lucky enough to be around at the time.

I blink. The looters continue looting. They howl at the night sky and bask in the drugstore's glorious conduction currents.

What am I talking about?

I shake my head and turn around, and I find myself face-to-face with a man who is not a man. A man with eyes—eyes not belonging to this world.

Eyes.

White, pearly eyes.

I scream, attempting to back up only to trip over my own damn funny bunnies. I fall flat on the ground, head smacking against the road. But it doesn't matter. Nothing matters. I'm gone. Drifting, drifting, gone . . .

I can't move. I can't think.

His face. White. White like a ghost. Skin smooth and ancient and eyes like something that should not exist. An elastic bio surgical mask is strapped around his mouth. He reaches to his face with bony, jagged fingers and pulls it off, letting it hang from his pencil-thin neck. He opens his mouth, revealing a set of teeth sharpened like knives. They are past the point of fangs. They are death. I do not want to see them. I do not want to see any part of this man. Of this creature. This death-maker. This soul-taker.

I can't move. Something's caught in my throat and I can't even choke on it properly.

He approaches, yet his feet do not seem to move, almost as if he's gliding. A white apron hangs down his chest, stained with smears of vermillion. He leans over me, but does not touch. His body slithers over mine, starting at the base of my funny bunnies and working his way up. He concentrates his toxic energy on his nasal passages. Smelling me. The fucker's *smelling me*.

As he glides further up, I am forced to stare into his eyes. I wish more than anything in the world that I could

34

be staring at anything else. Anything at all but these fucking eyes. Oh god. *These eyes.* I don't even think they are alive. No pupils detectable. All white, milky pears that— if given the chance—would not hesitate to devour all that I know and shit it back out as a giant turd of nothingness.

They are eyes that do not see like normal eyes see.

There are entire worlds in these eyes. Eternal voids eager to drown me, waiting for their chance to hold me prisoner in their own vacuum.

And then I realize he isn't just smelling me.

He's *breathing* me.

Breathing in my sweat. Breathing in my fear.

And it's all so clear.

I am his air.

His food.

I am his life force.

His provider.

I am his orgasm.

Any second now he will consume me and I will cease to exist. Forget my campaign to retrieve my identity. He will take me to a world where identity is no longer a concept. I will just be nothing and I'll be glad for it.

Take me . . .

And then he speaks, and all thoughts of enlightenment abruptly die.

A voice so old, so ancient, so haunting . . .

It's a miracle he can speak at all. It comes out as one raspy breath:

"*Oasis. Save Oasis.*"

And with that, he explodes into a cloud of ash.

chapter five

No, wait. Shit. Not ash.

Spiders.

A cloud of tiny black spiders drift toward the ground, replacing the ancient body of the white creature who had only seconds ago hovered over me. *Spiders?* Of course they're spiders. Anything less terrifying would just be breaking the rules.

I scream and back up, swatting the mischievous little fuckers off my coat. What the hell *was* that thing? Christ. *Spiders.* Crawling on the sidewalk, on the road, into the sewage drains. Crawling under my funny bunnies. I jump up and down, smashing them to death with my adorable footwear.

Whatever that thing had been, he did not belong to this world. Maybe he doesn't belong to any world—an outsider to all, a monstrosity to everyone.

Oh god, his eyes. So dead, so unnatural. So helpless.

Where were the pupils? Where was the *life?*

The problem is, there *hadn't* been any life. The creature had been blind. Hence the smelling. The breathing me in. He'd been using his other senses to drink in my appearance. To bathe in my fear. To analyze the inner workings of my mind.

Still, none of this explains what the holy hell that *thing* had even been.

Either way, he's nothing now. The spontaneous explosion pretty much took care of him. All I have to do is look down at the lake of spiders beneath me. I can feel them. On my skin. In my hair. My fingernails. Little flakes of spider guts caught in the corners of my eyes.

In my lungs.

Infiltrating my throat, clawing at the walls as they ride down into my intestines, poisoning my stomach with their grotesque plagues.

I gag and vomit onto the tiny little monsters. It makes a sickening sound as it hits the pavement, small flecks ricocheting back on my funny bunnies.

Glancing to the drugstore, I see the flames have progressed as much as I'd predicted. If anyone else is still in there by now, they're probably not going to be leaving. Not alive, anyway.

People flee the scene with overflowing shopping carts, rushing past me fuming with paranoia, as if any second they'll wake back up in the alleyway only to discover this all to be some wonderful dream. Others gather around the inferno, pounding their chests and bellowing fits of victory. Celebrating the destruction they've caused. Only it is not destruction in their eyes. It is art.

This is their masterpiece.

Mayhem at its finest.

This is what they consider beauty.

I must not belong to this particular group of people, because the scene only terrifies me.

But what if this isn't some particular *group*? What if this is how everyone behaves? What if this is life— *everywhere?*

I don't know what the fuck happened to me, but *something* seriously rewired the way my brain works. Nothing makes sense. Nothing seems natural. But this is the way life is. Why can't I accept it?

It hasn't been that long since I woke up at the river. How long could I have possibly been unconscious? Not too long, since the cops were using the car's GPS to track the location.

Who was I before the river?

37

A boy stares at me from across the street. Despite the looters returning to their aimless wandering, he still sticks out, as if the rest of these poor souls are mere mirages. He's the only other person besides me who's standing completely still. And, unlike the others, he actually seems to be *focused* on something.

Focused on *me*.

These other people seem to have lost all interest in everything. Even the excitement of the drugstore has already faded. The glow of apathy reflects in their eyes like a brick wall's reflection in a puddle.

But this boy here is different. He's looking straight at me. He isn't distracted by society, isn't consumed by some mystical zombie trance. He sees me and I see him.

I step forward. He steps back. Our eyes maintain contact. I move closer and he moves farther away, totally in sync with one another. I can't let him escape. He knows something . . . something that's going to help me. There's something about him I can't quite place.

I break from my calm stance into a dead sprint, pushing the street rats out of my way. The boy attempts to flee, but trips over his own untied shoelaces and goes sprawling on the sidewalk, face scraping against the pavement. I'm on top of him before he can react, grabbing him by the back of his black T-shirt and hauling him to his feet. The whole time all I'm thinking is: *please don't explode, please don't explode.*

"Get the fuck off me!" he screams.

No one stops to help him. I can do whatever I want to this boy. No one will intervene. But I don't want to hurt him. I just want his help. Yet I get the feeling all it'll take is one slipup for his head to suddenly go *poof*.

Please don't explode.

"Relax, kid." I tighten my grip around his shirt collar. "I'm not going to hurt you."

"Then let me go, motherfucker!"

"Not just yet."

"Aw, man, leave me alone." He tries his damnedest to wrestle away. I push him against the wall of a boarded-up building. His cheek slams against the bricks. "Stop, shit, stop! That hurts!"

"You gonna chill out then?" I bend his arm back about ninety degrees. He lets out a tiny squeal—totally overreacting, too. What a baby.

"Yeah! I'm chill! I'm chill!"

"Good." I ease the pressure off his arm. "Now tell me why you were staring at me like that."

"What?"

I grip his arm tighter but make no actual attempt to inflict pain. "You were staring at me. Why?"

"What do you mean, *why?* That dude was fucking crazy. Wouldn't you be staring too if some crazy fuckin' guy exploded like that?"

I pause, take a breath. "You mean you saw that?"

"That shit was nuts."

"So, you saw him . . . smelling me."

"Yeah, and then I saw him fucking explode. For some reason that part seems to have impacted me more. Crazy, huh?"

"Where did he come from? Do you know?"

"Shit, man, I don't know. One second he isn't and the next he is. The hell was that thing, anyways, huh?"

"Did you see his eyes?"

"What?"

"His eyes! Did you see them?"

"Nah." The kid shakes his head. "I was too far away. But I did see the part that you seem to be overlooking—you know, when he *fucking exploded?*"

I sigh. The kid's obviously no help. He doesn't seem to know any more than I do—at least, not about the creature that attacked me. I turn him around to face me, releasing my grip and hoping he doesn't try to make a run for it.

I pull the matchbook out of my trench coat pocket and hold it up so he can see the logo. At the glimpse of the matches, however, the boy immediately starts bugging out.

"Oh shit, oh shit, please don't set me on fire. Shit, man. Please."

I pause, thrown off balance. Like I could even set him on fire with a couple of lousy matches. Now, if I had some of whatever those people used to light up the drugstore, then maybe I'd be in business. Not that I'm planning on setting anyone on fire, of course. But it does always help to be prepared.

I shake my head at him. "What? Shut up." I wave the matchbook in front of him. "Do you know this place or not?"

"Of course I know it. Who do you think I am?"

"Someone with a memory."

"Yeah, well—uh," he pauses, contemplating, and goes, "yeah, I guess I am."

"Take me there."

"S'cuse me?"

"I want you to take me here." I tap the stamped THE RISQUÉ CABARET on the box around the cartoon pinup girl.

He laughs. "Oh okay, sure, just this way, mister . . . "

"I'm not screwing around, kid." I grab him by the shirt collar again. He doesn't seem to be as intimidated this time.

"Yeah, but I am," he says. "Now let me go, you fucker."

Surreally enough, I obey and unhand him. But then the satisfied smirk on his face becomes all too smug, and I snap out of my daze.

When I pull out the gun, all egotism quickly fades. I'm back in charge.

I push him against the wall. "What do you have to say now?"

I press the muzzle against his dark cheek and watch as the tears stream down his face. Hell, he's maybe fifteen at most. What am I doing? Am I really holding a gun on a child? For Christ's sake, he's about to piss his pants.

Why is no one stopping this?

How far can I take this before someone intervenes? If I pull the trigger, will anyone so much as bat an eyelash?

Would I be arrested?

I know what arrested means. I know shooting people in the face is exactly the type of thing that'd result in being arrested. But would anyone call the police? Would the police even care? Who's going to clean up this poor kid's brains from the wall once the ugly deed is done? How many people would I be able to kill before someone stopped me? Could I kill them all?

I could own these streets.

I could own this whole goddamn world.

These violent thoughts of mine, they make me shake, make me wonder what type of person I really am. But then again, maybe some things are best left unknown.

Maybe living the rest of my life in the dark isn't the worst fate. No one wants to live in the light. It gets too bright and gives you a headache. Light is bad news. The darkness is my friend. It understands my condition, and rather than emphasize my situation, it instead sings me a lullaby to help me forget all my troubles. Some things are best off locked in the cellar. This whole lost memory thing could be a blessing in disguise.

Either way, I now have somewhat of a hostage on my hands, and I must deal with him in an orderly fashion.

Note: don't make him explode.

Don't make him explode.

I wave the gun as menacing as I can and say, "Well, you gonna take me to this place or not?"

The kid tries to regain his cool posture. "Yeah, fine. I'll take you. But after you answer this one question. And you have to be honest."

I relax, returning the gun to my pocket. "Okay. Go for it."

The kid gestures behind me and goes, *"What the fuck is that?"*

Of course I look where he's pointing, and of course there's nothing remarkable. When I turn back around, the kid is halfway down the street, blending in with the rest of the vagabonds.

Well, shit.

chapter six

I'm left with two choices. One, I chase after the kid—or two, I let him go and continue trying to find this club by myself.

I'm sick of being by myself.

I push a naked cross-eyed man to the ground and sprint into the sweaty, disgusting mass of pedestrians. Thankfully he isn't too short, and I can see his shaven scalp bouncing above the sea of heads. I follow it, not caring whose feet I step on. It's their own fault for not getting out of my way fast enough.

I can't tell if the funny bunnies are helping or slowing me down. I consider ditching them, but at this point, it's almost as if they're a part of me now. The thought of losing them sends a shiver down my spine. Instead I push forward, eyes wide and on the watch for the kid's bouncing scalp.

I shout for him to stop but my voice is drowned out by the city's noise pollution. The kid's head disappears, and I'm certain I've lost him. I'm back by myself, left to find this club alone, left to wander this place forever, never finding any answers, never coming any closer to cracking this enigma that is my brain.

(her hand wraps around my hand and we both squeeze lightly, just enough to feel each other's presence. her nails are red, not red like fire but red like sweet cherries, red like comfort, red like warmth, red like home. her hand squeezes in a way that tells me i will never be

alone, that she'll always be here for me and everything will be okay, but when i look up, her face is blocked by her long red hair, red like her fingernails. 'i want to see you,' i say, and she tells me all i have to do is open my eyes.)

The kid scrambles over a sleeping vagrant on the sidewalk and flings himself into an alley opening. I head for the same direction, but a woman grabs onto the back of my coat collar and pulls me to the ground. She stands above me, her breasts sagging down to her knees and then slapping against my chest as she kneels. Drool drips down her mouth as she points accusingly.

"You!" she screams. "Give me your soul! Give me your soul *right now!*"

"Jesus Christ," I cry out, and kick her off me. She goes tumbling backward, somersaulting across the pavement. She screeches as strangers trample her. I climb to my feet and rush past them all, continuing toward the alleyway.

I pass a dumpster and stop, retreating back to the container. I consider getting my gun back out, but fear accidentally pulling the trigger in the heat of the moment, so I leave it in my pocket. I reach up and slowly push the dumpster lid open, peering inside. "You in there?"

"Piss off!" a voice returns from inside.

"Can't you see we're busy here?" another voice says.

"Hey, he's kind of hot. Wanna join?" a third voice asks.

I apologize and quickly close the dumpster. Gross.

Farther down into the alley I discover a featureless steel door. A filthy, shaggy man sits in the dirt next to it, leaning against a pile of bricks. A rubber tube tied in a tourniquet hangs loosely from his bicep.

"Hey," I say, and gesture to the door. "Did you see a kid go in there a few seconds ago?"

The man grunts, then spits a glob of something purple out. "Last time I saw anything, the devil himself was above me. Devil says, 'Johnny, you done been a bad boy, Johnny, you gonna pay for your misdeeds. Johnny,' he says, 'you gonna jerk off fire and shit maggots.' And then I see no more."

He spits again.

Everyone in this city is a goddamn lunatic. I move past him and open the door. The smell of something foul and toxic punches me in the face and knocks me a few steps back.

The man on the ground squeals with laughter. "Only thing in there's Conundrae ready to bite yo dick off and shove it up yo ass."

"Well, I guess I'll take my chances." I inhale a great gust of air and enter the building. The door slams shut behind me, trapping me in darkness.

I wave my hands wildly in front of me and walk forward, following the sound of hurried footsteps. I assume it's the kid still running away, but realistically it could be just about anybody. Or anything. After the pale spider creature, nothing is impossible.

I come across a staircase. I fumble for the handrail and climb, my grip around the wood so tight it's probably turning my knuckles white. Anything could be here in the shadows, waiting for me. A beast with an unhinged jaw might be resting at the top of the stairs, just hanging out until I walk straight into its mouth. Or I could be walking into nothing. The building could be empty. The kid might already be gone. Or the kid might not exist. Maybe none of this exists. I am still unconscious back at the river. This is all a dream. A hallucination conjured by a damaged mind.

"What the fuck did you think you were doing, huh?"

The voice brings me back to reality, back to the shadows. I suck in my breath and act like a statue. At the top of the staircase a gleam of light flickers. More than one person is up there. One of them's whimpering, almost crying. It's the kid.

"I . . . I'm sorry," he says. "I was being chased by a crazy person. I just ran into the first door I saw."

"Well, how convenient for you that you happened to see this door first, right?" a woman says. She giggles.

"I didn't see nothing," the kid says. "I swear to fucking god I didn't see nothing!"

A man laughs. "Boy, does this look like god's kingdom to you?"

Silence for a moment, then the kid screams out.

"I asked you a question. Does this look like god's kingdom to you?"

"N-n-no! *No!*"

"Then why you swearin' to him, huh? You actin' ridiculous."

"I'm sorry, I'm sorry, please don't cut me."

"Do it," the woman says. "Cut the little prick. No, wait, cut his prick *off*. We can play catch with it or feed it to Brutus."

The kid squeals.

"Nah," the man says. "Brutus has plenty of food from the last asshole we caught. This kid, I got something special in mind."

"Watcha thinkin', baby?"

"You know what I'm thinking."

"Conundrae?" the woman asks, and I swear I can hear the man nodding. She replies back with another heinous fit of giggling.

There's a lot of moving around, feet scuttling, something being dragged, and the kid starts screaming.

"No! What are you doing? *What the fuck are you doing?*"

"Oh, shut up," the woman says. "Consider yourself lucky. Not everyone gets to sacrifice themselves to a god."

I move forward, careful not to make the staircase creak as I step onto the landing of the second floor. I crouch behind a support beam, peeking my head out and watching the scene across the room. Small lanterns hang from the ceiling, barely shedding enough light to see. But what I *can* see is horrifying.

A man and a woman, both covered in sores and scars and pus, stand above the kid. The kid's flat on his back, limbs stretched out and tied to several hooks in the wooden floorboards. The man holds another of these hooks, softly pressing the tip of the blade against the kid's chest. Dismembered torsos hang by chains from the ceiling, next to the lanterns. Bizarre symbols are scribbled across the walls, accompanied with words like "CONUNDRAE" and "APOCALYPSE".

I gotta play it cool here. These people are clearly psychopaths. I need to sneak up on them, take advantage of the element of surprise. And, of course, just as I take another step, my foot breaks the floorboard beneath me. I try to wiggle free, but my funny bunny is so big, my foot's stuck between the wood.

Both of the psychos glance my way. "Now who the hell is that?" the man says.

"That'd be the crazy fucker chasing me," the kid says.

"And you *led him* here?" the woman asks.

"Holy shit, lady, do you not understand what the word 'chase' means?"

The man kicks the kid in the face, then looks back at me. "So, what do ya say? You feelin' up to being devoured by our great Lord and Master?"

"Well, uh, not really."

"That's okay. We don't actually need your permission."

"Then why'd you ask?"

"It's easier when you're agreeable."

I nod. "Makes sense."

The man and woman sprint toward me, the man holding up his hook and the woman holding out her long fingernails like claws. They're maybe five feet away from me when the floorboards crack again, only this time a much larger section of the wood disintegrates. Both the man and woman fall through the floor, to the ground level of the building.

I take a few steps forward and look down into the hole. They lay down on the floor below, motionless.

Well. That was a freebie.

I move around the hole, careful with my steps, fearing the same fate. I bend down and unhook the kid from his chains.

"Get up," I tell him.

He groans, slowly sitting. "You saved me, you fucking psycho."

"They did most of the work."

The kid points behind me and says, "Looks like we're still boned."

I turn around and spot a huge black dog growling at us.

"That must be the Brutus they were talking about," the kid says. "They were gonna feed that dog my dick."

"Nice doggie," I whisper, and the dog responds with a vicious bark. It springs at me and I jump to my feet, his snapping jaws missing my face by mere inches. I spin around and run at full speed in the opposite direction of the dog. It quickly gives chase.

"Nice doggie!" I scream, looking over my shoulder at the dog as I run blindly through the building. It occurs to me that the possibility of falling through the wooden floor is very high, but before I have time to really think about it, I instead run through a glass window.

I find myself flying in the night sky.

It only lasts a moment.

chapter seven

"Hey, man, you all right?"

For a moment I think I'm back at the river. But when I open my eyes, the kid is standing above me, extending his hand down. I reach up and take it, grunting as he pulls me to my feet.

"Shit, man," the kid says, "that was a long fall. I'm surprised you're still alive."

I look up at the busted window three stories above us. The shard of glass sticking in my shoulder stings like hell, but I'll live. I pull the glass out and drop it in a puddle, then crack my neck. Next to us is the dog. It unfortunately didn't have the same sort of luck as I did.

I nod to the end of the alley. "Well, take me to this club."

The streets have returned to their own little bizarre normality. Keeping a careful eye on my new guide in front of me, I try my best not to grunt or limp. I twisted my ankle something fierce on the fall down. Plus if the patch of warm wetness on my back is any indication, I didn't catch all the glass shards in my flesh during my initial inspection.

It's amazing how loud the night is, yet when I look around, no one is saying anything. Even the crazies shouting about the end of the world have quieted down. The noise, it isn't coming from the voice of another human. This is the voice of despair, screaming its prized melody—backup vocals contributing to hoarse coughs and unstable shopping-cart wheels.

I quicken my pace so I'm alongside the kid and casually bump his shoulder. I clear my throat. "Uh, hey."

"Uh, what?"

"What's your name?"

"Aerosol," the kid says.

"What?"

"*Aerosol.* That's my name. Aerosol. Peeps call me Aero, though. Not that you're a peep, of course. You see, peeps don't hold people at gunpoint and make them do shit they don't wanna do. Crazy fucker. I know people who could decapitate you with a pair of fingernail clippers, just like *that.*" He snaps his fingers. "All I gotta do is give the word."

"What the hell is a peep? Why are you named Aerosol? That is a stupid name."

"Oh, I guess your name's so much better, huh?" he asks, clearly offended.

"I hope so."

"Well, what is it?"

"Guess."

"What?"

"Guess my name," I tell him. "Go ahead."

"Okay." Aerosol nods. "How about Dickhead?"

"Wow, good guess."

"Oh, shut up."

I smirk. "So, why do they call you Aerosol?"

"'Cause it's my name."

"Oh."

"Why do they call you Dickhead?"

"'Cause I am."

"Oh."

We walk awhile longer in silence, letting the city's depression seep into our pores and mix within our chemicals. The street never ends. Not once have we taken a turn, not even a slight curve—just one straight stretch of pavement, accompanied by boarded-up buildings along the sides.

No matter how hard I try to concentrate, all sense of

time seems to evaporate from my grasp. I try to keep track of how long we've been walking, but it's no use. Just as I think I've finally figured it out, Father Time pulls the rug out from under my feet. I briefly sneak a glimpse at Father grinning maliciously right before I fall into a colossal hourglass, shattering the walls and slamming into its epic contents. It does not take long before my body begins sinking into its innards. Caught in a slow, drawn-out panic, I feel the weight of my lungs swelling inside me, drowning in a sea of infinite sand. Each block could account for either five minutes or five days. Nothing will surprise me at this point.

"So, tell me, Dickhead," Aerosol says, "how much bacon did that piece end up costing you?"

"Bacon?"

"Yeah, man—bacon. I'm betting it was some crispy bacon, too, huh?"

"Excuse me?"

He waves his hand dismissively. "Man, never mind, just forget about it."

Of course I know what bacon is. Bacon is delicious. Bacon is good, yet at the same time, bad for your life force. So this means sometimes bad equals good—therefore, does that mean good sometimes equals bad? It's an equation I'll probably never understand. Does anyone? Maybe we're just expected to accept it and move on with our lives.

All this heavy thinking about bacon has reminded me of the headache refusing to go away. It may fade down a little, but it never leaves. Maybe it's here for good.

Another consequence of deep bacon ponderings: my stomach is growling. I lick my lips and think, *bacon.*

Apparently the pastry I'd eaten at the drugstore had not been enough to satisfy my hunger. I could eat a horse right now.

But no, that is a lie. I remember horses. Horses are wonderful animals. Who could possibly eat one?

Shit, who knows. Maybe I have before, sometime in my

dubious past. I briefly consider the ingredients inside a horse, wondering if perhaps one of the side-effects happens to be memory loss, then decide I have no idea what is inside a horse, nonetheless what they taste like.

Goddamn, I'm crazy.

I think about the bar of chocolate in my coat pocket, but I'd be uncomfortable eating it in front of the kid. He doesn't look like the most well-fed boy, but still, another part of me refuses to share my last bit of food. I'll just save it until I truly need it.

Truly need . . .

What do I need?

I need *her*. Whoever she is.

She is my chocolate.

The answer to my hunger.

(under the blanket it's so warm, warm and safe, warm and safe because she's under here with me, our heads sticking out like content turtles. i feel our cold feet around each other, and they're so nice, so perfect. i know i want to be here forever. i want to stay. let me stay. the tv is on but i do not know what is playing, i'm more focused on the amazing energy her soft breaths generate. the recently opened box of chocolate candies resting on the sheets in front of us offer opportunity. i reach for one the same time she does and our hands connect, and it feels so right and we know that it isn't chocolate we need but each other, and soon the chocolate is out of our minds completely and all we know is ourselves—our wonderful warmth. her red hair falls into my eyes, temporarily blinding me, and by the time i am able to brush it away she is no longer in my arms and the box of chocolate is empty.)

"So I have to ask," Aerosol says.

"Ask what?"

"What's with the slippers, bro?"

"Um."

Short rapid pixels of violence flash before my eyes: my

hand raw, my headache throbbing, his skull disintegrating, his brains splattering, his face destroyed, life snipped short.

"Well?"

"These are my funny bunnies," I tell him.

"Yo, those are pretty tight, I gotta admit. Can I have them?"

I shake my head. These are *mine*.

He doesn't press the issue any further, and soon thereafter we finally come across the first twist within this deranged stretch of road. And sure enough, as soon as we make the holy turn around this deteriorating building that a hobo wouldn't even use to piss on, we find ourselves standing face-to-face with a large neon sign of a woman twisting her metallic nipples. She's propped up on top of a wide two-story building, glassy legs spread to the sky, revealing the words "THE RISQUÉ CABARET" welded between her thighs.

Aerosol claps me on the back. "We're here."

I turn to give him a word of thanks but the kid is already fleeing away from me like a bat out of hell. He looks over his shoulder and shouts, "Thanks for saving me, Dickhead!"

Then he is gone.

It's all right. His job is finished. Now it's my turn to lead.

My turn to get things done.

chapter eight

The neon sign lights up half the block, revealing a whole new set of doubtful citizens in its dubious spotlights. Drunks and junkies loiter around the carless parking lot, moving in a sluggish circle. It's like they're caught in some kind of surreal cycle of apathy—shooting up, puncturing veins, vomiting, stumbling, rinsing and repeating. It's a marvel they're able to stay on their feet so long.

Rock music overshadows the area, sneaking out from inside the club. The vocals are incomprehensible, but the heavy instrumentals are heavy and rude. If it's this loud outside, then inside my eardrums are in for one hell of a ride.

My eyes become lost in the sign's hypnotic glow, filling me with a sense of curiosity and showering me with fright. Each flicker taunts me further, egging me on and overwhelming me with a recharged gust of excitement. Beyond these robotic titties lies a series of answers that will hopefully reveal my identity: who I am, what I've done, where I've been, who I represent, what the hell's going on . . .

Because, really. What the hell *is* going on?

A muscular man stands behind the rosewood door at the front of the club, arms folded across his chest, pectoral muscles basically ripping out of a tight black T-shirt. His expression maintains the same mean eyes and pissed-off snarl.

He looks down with his angry, hateful eyes. "I've been wondering when you were gonna show up."

"Yeah, me too."

He stares at me for a moment like he's trying to murder me with his eyes, then his serious glare cracks and he starts giggling like a little kid. "What the devil you wearin', boy?"

I feel my cheeks blushing red. I look down at my feet, then back up at him. "Um, these are my funny bunnies."

"They are off the *hook*."

"Thanks."

"I am lying. That was a lie. They are horrible."

"Oh."

He motions to the front door. "You know the drill."

"Yeah." I nod. "I know the drill."

I move past him, take a deep breath, and enter The Risqué Cabaret.

Inside: Bright red seizure-inducing strobe lights flashing, spotlights zooming across the carpeted floor and catching unsuspecting junkies in its glare. Women dance in scarce clothing, swinging from cages dangling from the ceiling. Others grind against poles attached to tables. The men outnumber the women easily. They're slumped in chairs circling the stripper tables, while some lurk around the cages, their eyes following the dancing goddesses in an enthralled rhythm of false spirituality, tongues drooping from their mouths, hands rubbing their own crotches on the outsides of their pants and trying their best not to let anyone else notice. Those tired of watching the dancers doing their thing have skulked over into the forgotten shadows by the main bar, washing away their shared sorrows with poison.

This is their ritual. This is their life.

A couple dozen twentysomething-year-olds drunkenly sway on the dance floor off on one side of the room, minds already in their last stages of decomposition.

This is how we lose ourselves. This is how we forget.

But this is only short term. This isn't how I forgot. Something happened to me. Something bad.

Something that didn't happen on some lousy dance floor.

A select few sit off in the corner, playing a game of cards. From the sounds of their angry ramblings and intoxicated accusations, it's only a matter of time before a fight breaks out. All it's going to take is one word to set them all off, and then everything will turn to hell. One word—like, possibly, "cheat".

Now that I'm inside, the rock music is easier to hear, and the words sting my ears whether I want them to or not. I step over a couple of unconscious drunks and find an empty seat at a stool next to one of the pole dancers, burying my face in my own sweaty palms. The music and strobe light combination absorbs into my brain, soaking itself in me as if I'm just some human-sized sponge, multiplying the pain. My limbs weaken and I surrender my arms to the long table, tucking my head beside my armpits, falling prey to fatigue.

"You want this or not?"

Caught off guard, I straighten my spine and discover a waitress in a low-cut skirt beside me, hip cocked, one arm placed on her side, the other extending toward me with a dark bottle of beer in her hand.

"Oh, okay, thanks." I take the bottle from her and she's gone before we can negotiate payment.

I shrug and spin back around on the stool, directing all attention to the redhead working a number on the pole attached to my table. The table is long, crafted for more than just a couple of occupants. At least seven other men sit around it, stools pulled up, drool trickling down their unwashed chins.

The stripper's attire consists of nothing more than a black bra and panties. Red flames are stitched along the embossed edges. Her fingernail and toenail polish match perfectly with the lingerie. Her lower back houses a well-detailed butterfly tattoo.

And then her eyes.

So green, almost magical. It's as if they're the exact opposite of the bizarro surgeon's lifeless eyes back at the drugstore. His evil, hers good—so very good. A pair of eyes sent to show me the way to all that is right, to all I've forgotten that I secretly wish I hadn't. These eyes—so green, so striking, so safe. They fill me with this strange, wonderful sense of déjà vu, a feeling I've been yearning all night.

The waitress had already popped the lid off the bottle before serving it to me, so all I have to do is squeeze the opening between my lips, tilt my head back, and enjoy as the cold liquid caresses my throat. It tastes so damn good that I get the urge to pound my fist against the table and howl like a maniac.

Within one swift motion I empty the bottle, and I'm already thinking how much I want another. Fuck ibuprofen. Beer is all I need. I know beer. Beer is good. Yes.

But the waitress is nowhere in sight, so I push the empty bottle aside, readjust myself on the stool, and belch. The music breathes into my ears and sweeps me away with the dancing goddess in front of me.

This Lamb guy is taking a long time to find me. What am I even going to ask him? My mind is a tornado of unsolved puzzles. Half the pieces are missing, claimed by some unknown force.

There's a good chance he'll shoot me in the face upon sight.

I don't know him, at least not anymore. But he still knows me.

He might even know the dead thug back at the river. Maybe the thug was one of his employees. Fuck, I don't know. This whole universe is a mystery. Questions like haystacks and answers like needles hidden in the questions. Everything is under my nose but out of my sight.

Who am I?

But that's not the most important question anymore.

First I want to know if I even want my life back, because so far, I don't want anything to do with this shit. If this lifestyle is the real me, then I am a monster.

I'm not supposed to be a monster.

The redhead on the table begins making her rounds from customer to customer. They all dig into their pockets for dollar bills whenever she gets close enough. She's moving closer to me, and I realize I don't know what to do when she eventually arrives. I don't have any money on me. I have a gun, but I don't think she wants to see that. I have a chocolate bar. But why should she have my candy? Fuck her, I'm saving that for later. What if I find myself trapped, isolated from all of humanity, and that chocolate bar determines whether or not I live or die?

Oh crap, here she comes.

Before I know what I'm doing, the chocolate bar has mysteriously transported from my coat pocket to my hand, and I'm shoving it toward the stripper's bare flesh. "Take it, take it, it's all I have. *Take it.*"

"Cute." She smirks. "If only you had a Klondike Bar, then maybe you'd get some head."

"I will get this Klondike Bar."

She brings her hand close to my face, gently rubbing my stubble. "Don't forget Ezzy's diapers, either."

('da-doo da-doo wake up da-doo wake up')

"Huh?"

She giggles. "What are you wearing? It is so *sexy*."

"What?"

We're interrupted by the rest of the horny men at the table. Some whistle, others punch the wood, trying to get the girl's attention.

"Hey, lady," one of the guys says, "there's other people here, too, ya know. Jesus Christ, one asshole walks in with funny bunny slippers and all the chicks go crazy. It's just like my junior prom all over again, I swear."

Another one says, "Yeah, I got a Klondike Bar for you, sugar tits. What would you do for it?"

More whistles and applause follow.

"Gotta get back to work," she says, and gives me a quick kiss on the cheek. "Catch ya later tonight. Wear the slippers."

And with that, she's off rubbing her breasts in some other guy's face.

"Okay, will do . . . " I drift off with her warm lipstick smeared across my cheek. Then I blink. "Wait—what?"

I stand up, trying to get her attention, when a large hand—*paw*—clasps down on my shoulder and spins me around to face him. It's the same huge bastard who'd been standing guard out in front of the club.

"*What?*" I scream, scared out of my mind. Don't have a mind.

"Mr. Lamb will see you now."

"Oh. Uh, cool."

I glance back over my shoulder, wishing I had some extra time to speak to the girl on the table. But maybe after this is over, she'll still be waiting for me.

I can only hope.

I turn back to the bouncer. "So, where do I go again?"

He gives me a puzzled look, nods to the right, grunts, and returns back to his post outside.

"Oh, uh, right. I knew that. Carry on."

I return the chocolate bar to my coat pocket and head toward the direction he'd gestured, soon arriving at a steel door attached to the wall beside the bar. I slip inside to an old, isolated stairway, following the steps up to the next landing. Upon entering the next floor, I find myself standing in a small, darkly-lit office.

There's a desk visible at the back of the room, thanks to a long-necked goose lamp placed on the surface. It's the only thing in the room lit well enough to be observed.

A ball of dark blond dreadlocks joins the rest of the crap on the desk, sliding across a black tray in a horizontal motion and shooting up into a more professional sitting position. A face emerges from within the snakes. The crooked powdered nose attached to the face wiggles exotically from the aftershock of the snorting session. The dreadlocked man cracks his neck and roars like a lion.

"Now that's what I call motherfuckin' pure!" He stomps his foot on the floor and pounds his fist on the desk.

I remain standing there until his dilated pupils finally notice my existence. His expression brightens dramatically.

"Bob! It's about damn time! I thought maybe someone had killed you again."

(interlude i)

the office is gone. the man with dreadlocks is gone. the world is gone.

i am gone.

darkness. total, enriching darkness.

a cold drift arrives, but it is a welcomed breeze, as if before its arrival my flesh had been sizzling to the bone. but now it is all better. the draft soothes my nonexistent skin, makes my phantom legs form an impossible smile. i may be gone but i am still here, just not there.

my mind survives—my body, on the other hand, is off doing its own thing in some other dimension. it's okay, i don't need a body. i don't need a thing except for this heavenly wind caressing my soul.

it's goddamn erotic.

then i orgasm, and i'm forced out of this wonderful darkness and cast back into reality.

only the office and the man with dreadlocks are still gone. instead of the risqué cabaret i'm now standing in a bright hallway. my legs are asleep and don't last long before collapsing from underneath me.

slowly but surely (sugar pie) i climb back up this green abstract wallpaper until i've returned to a sturdy standing position and have a chance to browse my surroundings.

a man stands in front of me, who shares basically an identical height and weight, only this guy is a little less brawny than myself. in front of him waits more men and women, all standing straight and still, hands folded behind their backs. when one person steps forward, the rest of them follow. there is no delay in their movements— they are in perfect unison.

i glance over my shoulder, expecting to find more people waiting in line behind me, stepping behind with the rest, but i'm instead overwhelmed by a deep ocean of darkness. the same darkness my spirit had previously been swimming—drowning—in. i'm tempted to leap back into its vast beauty just to lose myself and forget about everything. it's where i need to be, where destiny is guiding me.

but despite how hard i try to move, i am unable to retreat a single foot away from the man in front of me. every step he progresses forward—no matter how slight— automatically expands the black wall of nothingness and pushes me after him like some kind of surreal escalator.

i reach out and tap the man on the shoulder, but he refuses to acknowledge my touch. every few seconds there's a brief change in line. we're all moving, and no matter how much i try to stay still, i can't. it's no use. it's as if there's an invisible chain hooked to the back of him and the front of me, and i'm just being dragged along to enjoy the ride.

i try to open my mouth to speak but my lips are sewn together. thick stitches replace all character in my lower face. i frantically claw at my mouth, prying my jaw apart, and after a while it finally shows a sign of tearing— skin stretching like silly putty.

breathing heavy, i exercise tarnished vocal cords and plead for him to stop.

"HEY!" i scream, and a wave of sound is clearly visible as it departs my mouth, drifting off into the air and soon evaporating near the ceiling.

no one hears me. i might as well not be here.

the hallway seems just as long as the street back out in the city, with the rest of the zombies. i go with the flow *for a little while longer until we finally reach a tall titanium door. beside the door resides a table with a man sitting down behind it, typing away at a computer. the man wears a dark blue robe, and the word that comes to mind is 'indigo'.*

indigo . . .

there are only three others in front of me now, and i'm finally able to hear what the man is saying to them.

'you are now brother bloodgood,' he says. 'welcome.'

the first guy steps through the door and it closes before i get a chance to see what's on the other side.

the next one in line approaches the table and the man behind the computer brushes his fingers across the keyboard for a moment. 'you are now brother slaughterfield. welcome.'

the next guy in line, the one in front of me, steps forward. i join him next to the table.

i clear my throat and say, "sup.'

the man at the computer hops on the bandwagon with everyone else and utterly ignores my existence. jerk.

he instead does his little thing on the computer and says, 'you are now brother bob. welcome.'

bob?

'bob?' the man beside me echoes. 'are you serious?'

the man in the indigo robe nods and gestures to the door.

'what kind of name is that?'

he shrugs. 'it's a name.'

'a pretty pathetic name is what it is.'

'it's a fine name. my uncle was named bob. he was a good man.'

'compared to bloodgood and slaughterfield? *yeah, it fuckin' rocks, dude. super tough.'*

'oh, come off it,' the man says. 'i don't choose the names, now do i? it's all the computer's doing. now move on, will ya?'

brother bob sighs. 'can't i just pick my own?'

'well, all right. what do you have in mind?'

'uh, i dunno.' brother bob scratches his head. 'baby puncher? dick steel? uh, shredder? any of those would be great.'

'hmm.' the man hovers back over his keyboard, typing away. 'all of those are already taken, sorry.'

'even baby puncher?'

'sorry man, what can i say? you should have gotten in line sooner.'

'well, shit.'

'what about chad? that one's available. it's pretty hardcore.'

'oh, screw you.'

brother bob heads through the door. i try to follow, but the chain that's been connecting us all this time must have snapped. gravity pushes me back into the darkness, falling, falling, drowning . . .

some unknown deity flips off the lights and the hallway vanishes. it is here, floating in merciful darkness, that i realize who the man is, the one labeled 'brother bob'.

the man is me.

chapter nine

I continue freefalling in this universe devoted entirely to darkness when, without warning, I'm back upstairs at The Risqué Cabaret. Not even a second has passed since the dreadlocked man spoke my name. I'm still in mid-blink. The fly orbiting around my head hasn't moved in a century. Then someone hits the PLAY button, and life shoots back into real time.

"Eh, Bob?" The dreadlocked man snaps his fingers. "You all right there, buddy?"

I clear my throat. "Uh, you're calling *me* Bob, right?"

He nods. "I believe so, yes."

I slowly point at him. "And you're . . . Lamb, right?"

"Correct."

"Cool." I tap my fingers along the hems of my trench coat. "I have some questions I've been wanting to ask you."

Lamb raises his brow. "Yeah," he says, "I've got some questions for you, too."

I hold out my hands, forming a shield. "Before you even ask, these are my funny bunnies, and no, you cannot have them."

"Judging from the look in your eyes, you ain't in the mood to play no games," Lamb says, grinning, "and that's a damn fine thing, because guess what? I ain't in no mood to be playing no games, either."

I nod.

The gun in my trench coat sags down, tugging at my shoulders and stretching out the fabric. One minute from now, the gun could be in my hand, and Lamb could have a hole in his skull. Maybe less than that. Or maybe he'll have the gun and I'll have the hole. Goddamn this world.

"Good, I'm glad we're on the same page here," Lamb says. "Now, the way I see it, we both got ourselves some questions. You're probably wondering why you woke up at the river—and, well, I'm kind of wondering why you woke up at all. It's not every day I look at a ghost, ya know? All right, so here's what we're gonna do. We'll play a little game. I'll ask a question and you answer, then you ask, and I'll answer. Sounds fair?"

I maintain my silence, fearing a single blink could kill any masculinity I may be radiating at the moment.

"And the game will stop once we've come to a settlement, or the other is dead. Preferably you. Maybe this time you'll die right."

"What's that supposed to mean?"

Lamb wags his finger. "Ah, ah, ah, you'll have to wait your turn."

I glare at him, waiting for him to ask me something.

A full minute passes before he says, "Where's the package, Bob?"

"What package?"

Lamb slams his fist against the desk and a cup of writing utensils tips over. "The *heart!*" he screams. "*Where is my heart?*"

The sudden maniacal tone is so unexpected and unsettling that I realize this is not a man I want to tempt, because he will bite, and he will bite hard.

But something inside me, some smartass demon locked in a cage deep within my spirit, can't resist pounding on the bars a little and making a goofy face at this wild animal. "Uh . . . in your chest?"

Lamb doesn't flinch, but still somehow signals a man

hiding in the shadows to leap out of his corner and elbow me in the side of my skull. The triggered headache is instantaneous.

I manage to stay standing and turn toward him.

"Not cool," I say, and spit in his direction. My aim isn't too shabby: the glob of saliva hits him dead in the face. The bodyguard responds with another elbow, this one slamming into my gut and doubling me over. I collapse on one knee, my hands pounding against the floor. He is one big son of a bitch, I'll give him that.

That had also not been cool, but I suppose I can let it slide this time.

Although a part of me wants to bring out my gun and blast a hole in him, show them all who's boss. Blow that obnoxious brute's pretty little face off his big, stupid skull. Then turn around with that magnificent chunk of steel still in my hand, shove the barrel down Lamb's throat and make him suck on it. And after I've found out all I want to know, I'll squeeze that glorious trigger and sing hallelujah to the Lord.

Or fuck that. I could just use my weird mind powers and disassemble them all into a hundred different pieces. Assuming I know how to control it, which I clearly do not.

I clear my throat and shake away the evil thoughts, standing back up and ignoring delicious temptation. "Sorry."

"It's okay," Lamb says, disturbingly calm. "You were just a little fuzzy on the rules, ain't that right?"

"Yeah." I scratch the back of my head and wince . "That's right."

"And we're ready to play for real now, yeah?"

"Yeah."

"Good, good." Lamb rubs his hands together. "Now, Bob, please answer me this: where the fuck is the package? It's kinda important to me, ya know, retrieving these particular items just so happens to be the one key thing my job's relied on to fulfill. And if I was to lose one of these, uh, shipments . . . well . . . needless to say, I am gonna end up hearing it out the ass from my boss, from *your* boss, and let me tell you something, Bob—I really, really dislike hearing things out of my ass. In fact, I don't particularly care for anything coming out of my ass except for shit and the occasional goldfish, but that's my own personal preference and I understand not everybody's gonna agree with that, and don't even start preaching your goddamn goldfish rights crap at me, because I've already heard it all. The point is, I don't care. I've always done what I liked and I am gonna continue to for as long as I'm alive. Understand?"

"Um."

"Okay, disregard that last part," Lamb says. "What I'm trying to say is this, protecting that package is my motherfuckin' job, right? Well, I really, really like my job. Don't you think it'd be a real shame if I lost it? This city ain't exactly excelling in the job market these days, in case you haven't noticed. What's a man to do if he ain't got no cash flow? He might as well not even live. Just be another one of those pathetic fuckin' ghouls out there in the pits with their sad little shopping carts. I'd be better off blowing my own goddamn brains out right here and now, don't you think?"

I'd be very glad to oblige you with this, I want to say, but I keep my mouth shut.

"And of course, I don't want to go blowing out my goddamn brains. Just a big ol' needless mess for Raoul here to clean up, and boy let me tell you, Raoul *hates* cleaning up blood."

"Especially brains," the man in the shadows adds.

"*Especially* goddamn brains." Lamb slams his palm against the desk, getting more and more worked up. "So, Brother Bob, you gonna tell me where that heart is or am I gonna have to blow my goddamn brains out? Not before, of course, blowing out yours, as well. And don't tell me you don't know because I *know* you know. Hell, I got me eyes

68

all over this city, and these eyes are telling me they saw you enter *the place* and leave with the package in your possession. During this time, one of my own men was murdered and the building burned to the ground. I gotta assume you are responsible. But I'll worry about all that crazy shit later, because priorities are priorities. Thus, the question remains: what the fuck did you do with my motherfuckin' heart?"

It takes me a moment to realize he's quit talking. I clear my throat, searching for the right words to say, but every possible answer feels like it'll end with *someone's* goddamn brains blowing out of their skull. To be fair, I haven't seen any of these two with an actual gun, but assuming they aren't packing would be extremely foolish.

"It was stolen," I tell him. Lying is not going to get me anywhere. "Stolen by a maniac in his dirty underwear."

Lamb stares at me for a moment, at a loss for words, and nods. "I see," he finally says, clapping his hands together. "Well, that certainly sucks."

"Yeah."

"I was really hoping that wouldn't be the case, Bob, but you know what I'm gonna have to do now."

"Um."

"That's right, Bob." Lamb stares into my eyes. "I'm gonna have to kill you. Again."

"Oh."

"Only this time, I'm gonna blow your goddamn brains out. And then I'll probably blow out my own, too—because, I'm just as screwed as you are right about now. The only difference is, you aren't gonna get the pleasure of killing yourself a sorry sonofabitch before it's all said and done with, unlike *moi*. But, don't worry now, I'm a pretty fair guy. This is a game, after all, right? And I do believe you deserve a turn."

Lamb grins.

"And make it a good one," he says, "'cause it's gonna be the last question you ever ask, assuming you're allergic to bullets like the rest of the human race. And I'm gonna go out on a limb and say you are, aren't you?"

"Uh, it's not your turn to ask a question."

Lamb laughs and holds out his hands. "Okay, you got me there."

"Why did you kill me?" I ask him. "Er, try to, at least."

My eyes refusing to break Lamb's gaze lest he notice a change in my own concentration, my hand starts crawling down the side of my trench coat, slipping in the pocket and curling around the gun like a sly snake acquainting itself with a tree branch. On the inside, I manage to slow the speed of my heartbeat, but on the outside, I maintain the frightened little boy look, careful not to let him detect this redeveloped composure.

After some consideration, Lamb finally answers my question. "You really have no idea, huh?"

I slowly shake my head.

"Well, Bob, it's like this." Lamb leans forward. "You fucked up. And I mean, you *really* fucked up."

"Oh."

"You fucked up *big time*."

"I see."

"Yeah, if only you *did* see. But you don't see shit, do you? No, you don't. You have it all written across your poor pathetic face. Listen, Bob, trust me when I say that you screwed over the wrong people. I don't even know where to start. You know what we do here, what the main purpose is, yeah?"

My blank look is all of an answer I need to give him.

"Damn, that vac really screwed your shit up."

"What did you say?"

"Nothing, it's not important now." Lamb waves his hand dismissively. "But what you need to know is this: you work for me—or, at least, you did. Now, I ain't the boss here in the whole scheme of things. Hell, even Indigo himself don't call the shots, not when you think about who we *really* rule under, who it is we obey. Who we worship."

"Conundrae." The word leaves my mouth but the word does not belong to me.

Lamb grins. "What can you tell me about Conundrae, Brother Bob?"

This time, I have nothing to say. I shrug. I think about the crazies in the city with their posters and chants praising Conundrae, but what does it all mean? What does any of this mean?

"Shit, man," Lamb says, "is there anything you *can* remember?"

"Yeah, actually."

"And what's that?"

"I remember a river, and I also remember finding two bodies—one dead, the other nearly dead—keeping me company. I remember all that very clearly, but what I don't remember is how I got there, or why, or anything fucking else, so if you can please do me a favor and fill me in on this, that'd be pretty cool of you."

"Okay, okay—you wanna know why you were there?" Lamb pushes his hands off his desk as he stands up. "You fucked over the wrong people, Bob. A lesson was dealt, punishment was served. It's a tale as old as time, but this time it went wrong. It wasn't the first time the . . . operation failed, but it was the first time that someone woke back up afterward. And those two dead fools back at the river? Well, I knew one of those sons of bitches, and you just so happen to be wearing his coat. The cop, though? Well, you tell me, Bob. You fucking tell me."

It's surreal, standing here perfectly still while he loses it in front of me, voice rising with each passing syllable. Things are about to change. The conversation is dying. This room is going to be stained red.

"His name was Oasis," I say.

"Oh, is that so?" Lamb smirks. "How'd you know that?"

"The radio, in his car, it was calling for him. They used his name: Oasis."

"Anything else?"

"Well, he's dead. Your boy shot him."

"Yeah, and he shot my boy, so I guess they're pretty even, now ain't they?"

"I guess so."

"So what was he doing there, Bob?"

"What?"

"What was that motherfucking *pig* doing at the river?"

"I don't even know what *I* was doing at the river."

"You?" Lamb laughs. "You were supposed to be stayin' dead, that's what you were supposed to be doin'."

"I see."

"Yeah, and don't get me wrong now, Bob—we weren't *trying* to kill you. It just happened. Such are the risks when you attempt to reprogram a human being."

"*What?*"

Lamb reaches down at his desk, grabs a handful of the white powder spilled everywhere, and snorts it out of his palm. He returns his gaze back to me, smiling. "Hey, Bob, I hear you had a nice little run-in earlier with a renegade harvey. As I recall, you had just finished murdering my pickup boy, yeah?"

"What the hell are you talking about?"

"One of my sources tells me you and a harvey had yourselves a nice little chat. And word is, this was one of those nasty rebellious sons of bitches."

The creature with the surgeon's mask. The thing that'd exploded into spiders.

"What did you call it?" I ask.

"Har . . . vey."

"That was . . . its *name?* Harvey?"

Lamb pierces me with another sharp glare. "Short for *harvester,* you braindead retard."

"Oh."

"Now, tell me what you two talked about before he . . . whatever happened to him. These things never talk, Bob, so if it did to you, then it must've been pretty damn important."

('Oasis. Save Oasis.')

But Oasis is already dead. The harvey was too late. I'd killed him myself. But why would the harvey give a shit about a cop?

Why would the harvey give a shit about *me?*

('Save Oasis.')

What am I even doing here? The man has already promised to blow my brains out, for Christ's sake. The longer I stay here, the more I put my life in danger, and I'm just going to give this bastard the satisfaction of making up for his previous mistake.

His mistake being, of course, his failure to kill me correctly the first time.

And now I've returned to show him how it's done.

"You know, Lamb, there may be something I do remember that I neglected to mention earlier."

Lamb raises his eyebrow. "Yeah? And what might that be?"

"Well, you see, back at the river, there was something else I found there beside the two dead bodies. Something I took other than a lousy coat."

Still leaning against the desk, Lamb laughs. "Boy, if you think I don't know about that piece in your pocket, you is a goddamn fool."

Raoul shoves the barrel of a pistol against my ribcage as he takes my own gun from my pocket.

Shit. Shit. *Shit.*

"You honestly expected to walk all up in here packin' without me knowin' about it? Bitch, please. Raoul here has had his sights on you since you walked in the joint."

I wait for Raoul to pull the trigger. Lamb is still monologuing, but I've stopped listening. The man only talks to hear himself speak.

I close my eyes and concentrate. I think about the man behind me, waiting to kill me as soon as he's given the word. I think about the lamppost back at the park. It'd exploded at my command. I have the power. I am in control. I am the hero of my own shit.

73

Something behind me cracks and Raoul screams. The gun drops to the floor. "My wrist! My fucking wrist!"

I shoot my leg back, thoroughly crushing the bodyguard's unsuspecting nut sack up into his groin with the bottom of my trusty funny bunny slipper. His scream rises as he collapses on top of me, limp and helpless. I shake him off and he drops like a stone. He holds his arm up, revealing his wrist completely snapped in half. Multiple bones stick out of his arm.

Lamb is still standing where he was before, frozen. By the time he breaks his paralysis, I've already recovered my pistol. His eyes widen, and a moment later his lips stretch out to his ears, revealing only a faint hint of a sinister set of canines.

"Well shit, this is unexpected," he says. "And certainly impressive, I'll give you that. The last motherfucker to kick Raoul there in the balls and shove a gun in my face . . . well, I do believe you are the first one to attempt such a crazy stunt. Congratulations, Bob, I'll have to give Molly my condolences at your funeral."

(molly molly molly)

He pauses for a moment, letting his words sink in. "Oh, wait, there's not going to be a funeral, is there? All there's gonna be is you with a ton of bricks tied around your body, dragging yourself down to the bottom of the river where you should have been *hours* ago. But not to worry, good ol' Mol will still be there for me to give my condolences to. Right before she joins you with her own set of bricks. And don't think I've forgotten about that cunt of an offspring of yours, either. I doubt she's gonna need many bricks to get her little body to sink, though. Maybe a couple handfuls of rocks, huh? Shit, if that. One rock, two rock, three rock. 'Bye, 'bye, baby. 'Bye, 'bye."

I don't think—I just act.

The butt of the gun smashes into the side of Lamb's face and he goes flying against his chair, toppling over it to

74

the ground. It does very little to satisfy the anger seething through my veins, but it sure is a start.

The bodyguard attempts to stand up again, moaning at his shattered wrist, so I turn around and stomp my foot into his face, knocking him back down where I want him. I kick him a few more times and leap over to the desk. Lamb groans, confused. If I leave him here, he'll be after me before I even leave the building. He wants my blood. The sick fuck won't stop until I'm dead.

Or until he's dead.

He's done answering my questions, anyway.

I grab his dreadlocks and pull his head up, pressing the pistol against his jaw. He screams and tries to wrestle from my grasp, but it's useless.

Once the trigger's pulled and the blood's spilled, there's no fighting anything. There is only sweet surrender.

chapter ten

The sound of my funny bunnies slapping against the steps forms an echo in the stairwell, my heavy panting acting as backup vocals.

I leap off the last three or four steps and kick the titanium door wide open, the music from the club welcoming my reentry. Everything is still the same as it was before I left it earlier—hell, even the same redhead is up on stage, dancing some eternal dance. Only now she's lost the bra, her bare breasts swinging hypnotically with each sway of her hips. For a moment, I am unable to process any new information. Frozen, knowing I'm going to be discovered as a murderous psychopath any moment, and I just don't care. I can't take my eyes off her.

And then this jerk wearing a squirrel on his face in place of a mustache goes tumbling down in front of me, landing on a small round table and snapping it to pieces. I jump back, shaken from my reverie. Another man pounces on the squirrel man, punching him repeatedly in the face.

"You still think I'm a cheat? *Huh?* I'll cheat your face! With my *fist!*" yells the one doing all the punching.

"*Ahhhrrrgghhhhhaaa!*" yells the one getting punched.

I casually step over them and stride toward the redhead. She spots me and manages a sly hand wave in the middle of her dancing routine, and I briefly debate waving back. Then I realize how ridiculous that would make me look and I instead hop up on the table with her, knocking a few poorly-concealed erections out of their seats in the process.

The girl gasps, stepping back, although she makes no actual indication to flee.

"What the hell, Bobby?" she says, eyeing me like I've just done something totally outrageous.

Oh please, it was mildly strange at best.

I clear my throat. "Uh, hi."

"Hi . . ."

"So, um, how's it going?"

"It's going fine, Bobby," she says casually, placing her hands on her hips. "Now do you mind telling me what you're doing?"

"Er, me and you, we know each other . . . right?"

She cocks her head and smirks. "No, not all. I just screw every random guy who comes in here."

One of the drunks still sitting pounds his fist against the table and shouts, "Oh shit, what did I tell you, Mick? You owe me five bucks!"

Another patron goes, "Why don't you shut it, huh? She was obviously being sarcastic."

"Oh."

I lean in and whisper, "Were you?"

"What?" She gestures to her ears, reminding me of the music playing.

"Listen, you need to come with me."

"What's going on?" She stops dancing. "What's wrong?"

Over at the bar, the titanium door bangs open against the wall. I turn around just in time to spot Raoul rushing into the room, wielding a submachine gun in his uninjured hand. He scans the area for my whereabouts, so before I allow him the pleasure of spotting me on the table, I desperately dig into my coat pocket and pull out my own gun.

The gun shakes in my hand. I try to think of a quirky one liner to yell out, but nothing comes to mind, so I squeeze the trigger without saying anything. The gunshot steals the room's attention.

The bodyguard stays where he is, unfazed. That's because I came nowhere close to hitting him.

The squirrel-faced drunkard who'd previously gotten his ass handed to him by an equally intoxicated pugnacious card player, on the other hand, turns out to not be so lucky. He clutches his gut, mouth agape, a river of crimson flowing between his fingers, and collapses.

"Oh, shit."

Now, like everyone else in the club, Raoul knows exactly where I am. Well. Shit. Time to retreat. I tackle the naked redhead off the stage just as he swings his submachine gun in our direction and unloads a spurt of fire upon us. If I would have moved a second later, the both of us would have a few more orifices in our bodies than necessary.

We land on the ground hard, her body beneath mine.

"Uh, hi," I blurt out again.

"*What is happening?*" she screeches in my face, which is an understandable reaction, given the circumstances.

I grab her hand and lead her around another set of tables, crawling on all fours, careful not to accidently move into the bodyguard's target. Even though we're out of sight, it still doesn't stop the man from raining another hail of gunfire in our general direction. Beer glasses shatter inches from our heads.

"Get low!" I scream, not that anybody needs to be told that at this point.

People trample around in a frenzy, screaming and fleeing to the exit. Others hide behind tables, while some just stand there like they've forgotten how to make their legs work, until the inevitable happens and they are shot down for being in the way. Many of the strippers who were currently up on stage doing their rounds are rewarded with the same fate—now nothing more than chunks of dead flesh.

Man, this *cannot* be good for business.

The gunfire pauses as he reloads, and I spring up to my

feet, gun gripped tightly in both hands. He hasn't moved from the spot we last left him in, only now he's fumbling for another clip of ammo. I pull the trigger. A bottle of liquor explodes on the counter beside him, so I aim a little bit more to the right and try again. This time I am rewarded with a more promising outcome as a cloud of red mist sprays out from his shoulder. The bodyguard drops his submachine gun and stumbles back until he trips over a stool and goes tumbling down with it.

"Oh, shit! I got him! I got him!"

I probably shouldn't be as excited about this as I am, but screw it: I got him! Who's the king of guns? I am, that's who. Yeah, that's right, baby.

"Why did you shoot Raoul?" the redhead shrieks, clearly hysterical.

"Because he was trying to kill us?" I suggest, helping her to her feet. I grab her hand again and lead her toward the front door.

"Well why was he trying to kill us?" she asks.

"I may have kicked him in the balls."

We pour out the front door with the rest of the frenzy. She's too slow, though, and starts to drag behind. Then I remember that it is cold and she is naked, which includes a lack of footwear. The gravel paved road isn't exactly comfortable, even with my funny bunnies on, so I can imagine what it must feel like for her. I stop and throw her over my shoulder, despite her protests, and flee down the street.

A gunshot rings out from the club and a bullet zips past my head, exploding into the neck of another man ahead of me. I have to maneuver around his corpse to avoid tripping.

I increase my speed, my hand clamped tightly down on her ass to ascertain she doesn't fall.

It's for safety reasons only, I swear.

I run a few more blocks until I'm completely out of breath. No one else from the club is in sight, although the streets are still filled with the aimless vagrants that had been wandering around before. If any of The Risqué Cabaret's patrons are indeed still around, then the zombies must have converted them awfully fast.

I slow down, my legs feeling like rubber, and take a sharp right into the first blind alley I come across. I lower the fidgeting redhead to the ground, her bare feet slapping against the wet grimy concrete. She folds her arms over her chest, shivering from the bitter coldness of the night. I'm just grateful it's no longer raining.

"*What the fuck just happened?*" she shrieks.

"Hell if I know." I shrug. "That was pretty crazy, right?"

"*Crazy?* They were trying to kill you! What the *hell* is going on?"

"Uh, well, I don't exactly know. I guess they just don't like me?"

"They don't like you? What is that? *What happened?*"

"I don't know! Stop screaming!"

"Well what do you expect me to do? It's cold! I have no clothes on. And what the hell are you wearing, anyway? Do I even have a job anymore? I want to know what's going on, dammit. Tell me!"

"I don't know, okay? Just please calm down."

"Okay, I'm calm!" she yells in a tone that is anything but calm. "Now tell me why Raoul was shooting at you."

"I told you. I kicked him—"

"—in the balls. Yeah, yeah, I got that part. You know what I meant."

I sigh, shrugging again. "Um, well, I'm still not exactly sure. I guess they were upset that I wasn't dead from when they tried to kill me earlier today."

"*What?*"

I place a hand on her shoulder, doing my best to keep my eyes trained on her face and nothing more, although I sincerely would love nothing more in this world than to lower them a few feet down. "Listen," I tell her, "it is a very confusing time for me right now, all right? I have just as many questions as you do, and right now I would like very much to ask you one of them, if that's all right with you."

She breathes out a visible gust of air, shuffling her legs up and down. "Well, go ahead."

"Okay, uh, this may sound a little strange, but please just bear with me, all right?"

"All right . . . "

"What is your name?"

She looks at me as if I've just asked the most ridiculous question ever conceived. Then her expression changes when she notices the absolute terror across my face.

"Please," I whisper. "Just tell me . . . "

She gently caresses her finger along my cheek and brings my face down to her face, our lips embracing into a kiss that sends a nice warm feeling down to the very core of my soul—of my life force. It reminds me of home. Of safe, perfect tranquility. Here, her lips on mine, my life force tasting her life force, this is where I am meant to be. It's where I've always been meant to be.

And, standing here in the alleyway with her in my arms, I know this truth will never change. Not now, not ever.

She briefly breaks contacts, but keeps her face close to mine, so close that I am able to breathe in her perfume and revel in its lovely scent. I never want this moment to end. I want to live in her perfume, retire my mouth on hers and never move away. This girl is my home—if I've only been positive of one thing tonight, it is that. My home. My warmth. My fuel.

My life force.

Our breaths heavy and reassuring on each other, my

eyes locked into hers and her eyes locked into mine, she smiles and says, "Don't you know who I am?"

And this time, I do know the answer.

"Molly," I gasp. "You're Molly."

(interlude ii)

Molly brings her lips back against mine and i close my eyes, losing myself in her scent, the cold wind encouraging us into each other's arms.

and then i no longer feel the wind, the coldness, the lips—it's all gone. panicking, i open my eyes to find not only the girl out of sight, but also the alley in which we'd previously been standing in.

everything is dark.

like before.

then it evaporates, and a new world materializes. i find myself indoors, resting on a closed toilet, bright lights seeping through the cracks among the stall i'm trapped in. unable to fully comprehend the sudden change in my surroundings, i do what i assume any reasonable person would do in such a situation: i scream and fall off the toilet, my face landing next to a mechanism of pipes and splashing in a puddle of ancient piss.

yet, neither my face nor hair are wet. not even damp.

temporarily distracted by this supernatural event of urine, i slowly stretch my arm out and probe my finger in the puddle. it doesn't feel like how a normal puddle should feel. it's warm, almost hot, and thick, reminding me of wet cement. i can only twirl my finger around it for a moment before the task becomes too difficult.

and still, my finger remains dry.

i stand, using the toilet for balance, and wonder why i was just playing in a puddle of piss.

turning toward the closed door, i spot crude graffiti overwhelming the back of the stall, most of it fading away to near incomprehensible markings. in the dead center, however, there is a poem written in black permanent marker. it's fresh, as if just written:

as I sit
I contemplate
should I shit
or masturbate?

'where the hell am i?'
below that graffiti, it says CONUNDRAE WILL RISE. of course he fucking will.
i swing the door open and step out of the stall, finding myself in a regular public bathroom. a line of stalls identical to the one i've just exited wait behind me, a series of urinals mimicking its formation on another wall of the room. directly across from the stalls a sink hangs below a mirror, and in front of this sink stands a man hunched over, washing his hands.
'hey!' i shout, approaching the stranger. 'where am—'
i stop dead in my tracks as i spot the man's reflection in the mirror and realize there is no one standing there behind him. he is the only person in the bathroom.
yet i'm here, i know i am, so why can't anyone comprehend this?
i suddenly understand something else, too. this man, he's the same one from that hallway, the one named brother bob.
the man is me.
me #2.
he twists the faucet to OFF and turns around, coming face-to-face with myself. it's almost as if he stares straight into my eyes, but it still doesn't seem to faze him at all— not how it does me. he exits the bathroom, and i follow,

entering a bar. it's not as elaborate as the risqué cabaret, but it is a bar nonetheless. people are drinking, laughing, yelling. the kinds of things everybody does at a bar.

now we're at a pool table. me #2 twirls a pool stick in his hand like a cane. there's this certain smugness across his face that makes him stand out from the others. a growing crowd circles him and his friends, applauding as the game progresses.

'ten bucks says i get that 7 in the corner pocket there,' me #2 says.

'i'm in.'

'yeah, me too.'

me #2 cracks his neck, bends down, aims, and fires. he clears the table, save for the cue ball. another eruption of cheers burst from around us.

'i'm out.'

'yeah, me too . . . '

'i can't believe you made that shot, man.'

'what can i say? i have skill.'

'nah, it's just the luck of the irish, plain and simple.'

me #2's smile brightens. 'yeah, maybe so. now pay up, you cheapskate bastards. i gots me some more drinkin' to attend to.'

i stand by, idly watching as the 'cheapskate bastards' pay me #2, and then skulk off out of sight, cursing under sour breaths. a man with a tall green mohawk stays with us and collects some of the pay.

'they get dumber every day, don't they, bob-o?' he laughs.

'you'd think they'd learn,' me #2 says.

'nah, too much fuckin' booze, mate. us, we can drink all night and still play like the best of 'em. these fucktards, on the other hand, you give 'em two shots and they're done for. they'll wake up tomorrow broke, telling themselves they'll never drink again. we're like civil fuckin' servants, man, i kid you not. we're saving lives while making them look like complete twats. that's what makes this game so fun.'

the two men progress into a long session of drinking, which is then followed up by even more drinking. they sit at the bar, sharing incoherent ramblings of various brawls they'd participated in over the years. it is all surprisingly boring and hard to keep up with.

as the patrons go about their business, i discover something very strange, something i figure i should have noticed right off the bat. some of their faces . . . they're not how faces are supposed to look. sure, some are easy to make out—their expressions detailed to the bone—while others, on the other hand, are nothing more than blurry, pixelated beings sculpted into the shape of generic humans. a small minority are mere orbs hooked on the train of passersby, dragging against the rails of vulgarity.

i briefly entertain the idea that there's a chance these orbs are just like me—maybe this is what i look like. is it possible there are others trapped in this nostalgic film of my past? do they see me? what are they doing here?

what am i doing here?

'hold that thought, mate,' mohawk says, downing his beer and stabbing his cigarette butt out into an ashtray in one swift motion. 'gotta see a man about a mule.'

'why do you say that?' me #2 asks. 'don't say that. it is a stupid thing to say.'

'just tryin' to adapt to your american lingo, mate.'

'you've never been out of the states in your entire life.'

'yeah, but me old man visited london on a business trip once.'

'get out of here.'

'no, i'm serious, he really did.'

me #2 shakes his head. 'i mean, get out of here.'

'oh,' mohawk says. 'right.'

'and check out the verse i wrote in the middle stall,' me #2 adds. 'you'll get a kick out of it.'

me #2 remains hunched over the bar, oblivious to his doppelganger two stools away from him. then, finally, a *familiar redhead collapses down on the stool between us and shouts for a whiskey. the barkeep pours her a shot and she flings the warm liquor down her throat and is motioning for another one before he even has a chance to attend to the next customer. she looks very troubled.*

'you look troubled,' me #2 agrees.

'thanks,' molly says, soaking another fiery shot of whiskey into her liver.

'what's wrong?'

'nothing.'

'so there is no reason why you look so troubled?'

'i'm not. piss off.'

'but then why did you thank me?'

'i did?'

'yup.'

'right.' molly nods. 'now leave me alone.'

'someone's pretty feisty tonight.'

'i am through with men. i swear, if they all died tomorrow, it wouldn't be soon enough.'

'that . . . that's cool.'

'why are you still talking?'

'oh, um, sorry,' me #2 says, and goes back to sipping his beer in silence.

she slams yet another shot glass down on the bar and turns toward him. 'i mean, what is their problem? is there a sign pinned to my ass i am not aware of that says pinch here?'

'um, who is doing this?' me #2 timidly asks. 'i'll go pinch them in the ass, if you'd like. see how they like that.'

ignoring his nice gesture, molly smacks her palm down on the bar and exclaims, 'it's like one of the only rules, but can they follow it? huh? can their simple little dicks behave themselves? no, they have to touch.'

'well, i can't blame them.'

she looks at him unbelievably. 'i can't tell if you're trying to be sweet or you're just stupid.'

me #2 shrugs. 'can't it be both?'

molly eyes him for a minute and finally says, 'look, i may be a stripper, but don't go expecting any of my work life to mix with my social life. got it?'

'hey, we all gotta make a living somehow, right?' me #2 says. 'hell, i transport illegally harvested human organs. so trust me, i understand.'

the expression on her face is very queer. either she's about to burst out laughing, or she's going to get up and run away from us as quickly as possible.

luckily me #2 manages to break the tension before it has a chance to escalate: 'ha ha, relax, that was a joke. i was joking. i, uh, don't really do that. i am also a stripper, in fact. and i was just thinking how rude it is for all those women to be pinching my ass, too. i mean, really, a little common courtesy would be nice, am i right?'

'uh huh.'

'really, i'm telling you the truth here. i work over at the, uh, you know, the male strip club. whatever it's called.'

'studs n' muffins?'

'uh, yeah, that's the place.'

'they have the greatest muffins . . . '

the man with the tall mohawk springs out from the blurry faces surrounding us, excited about something.

'yo, bob-o, new fish, six o'clock,' he says, gesturing behind them in the general pool table area. 'c'mon man, let's get to 'em before some other cunt does.'

'dammit, rev!' me #2 says, struggling not to lose grip on his drink. 'you almost made me spill my beer.'

'yeah, yeah, whatever,' he says, prancing back and forth like a child with a secret. 'did you not hear what i said? new fish, bob-o, new fish!'

'yeah, i heard you,' me #2 says, gritting his teeth. 'can't you see that i am in the middle of talking to someone?" he pushes mohawk back a foot or two and nods to the redhead.

'why, 'ello there, darlin',' mohawk says. he gently picks up her limp hand and delivers a kiss to her knuckles.

88

'hello,' molly says, cautious.

'and to whom do i owe the pleasure?' mohawk asks.

'um,' me #2 says, clearing his throat loud enough to imply that he is still participating in the conversation, 'this is . . . um, wait, what is your name?'

she opens her mouth to reply but she is cut off by an eruption coming from the pool tables.

'oh, dammit, now do you see what we're missing?' mohawk snaps, pounding his hand on me #2's shoulder. 'new fish! stupid fish, by the looks of 'em. c'mon man, what are we waiting for? they're practically begging for us to take their money—and, uh, teach them a lesson on the dangers of drinking, of course. let's go.'

before me #2 has a chance to respond, mohawk is turning around to molly, offering his best smile. 'i apologize dearly for interrupting your, i'm sure, riveting conversation, lass, but as you can see there are some very important matters at hand here that we really must be attending to. you are welcome to watch, of course. in fact, it'd be our honor—isn't that right, bob-o?'

she appears to debate this for a moment, but ends up shaking her head, frowning. 'i should probably get going.'

and without another word, the girl spins off the stool and breaks into a solid stride toward the front door, leaving the three of us caught in a starstruck daze.

'man, just distract them or something,' me #2 says. 'give me a minute.'

me #2 leaps off his seat and races across the club, my own weightless soul pulling toward his movement with an expert magnetic touch. we run out of the building, leaving the bad music and rowdy drunks behind and enter a glowing night overthrown by an almost deafening silence. the only sound in the whole world is molly's distant footsteps clapping against the sidewalk.

we chase after her, begging for her to wait up, which she fortunately does by turning around and waiting

max booth iii

patiently next to a lamppost. we finally catch up, out of
breath and panting.

'yes?' she asks.

'uh,' me #2 stammers, straightening his back out.
'where are you going?'

'home, i'm going home. why? is that okay with you?'

'yeah, um, of course it is—why wouldn't it be? just, uh,
i thought we were having a good time is all.'

'i have to work tomorrow. go ahead and play your
pool. i'll see you around, slick,' she says, and attempts to
leave once again.

'can i at least get your name?' he asks.

she glances over her shoulder, and is that a smile on
her face? 'molly,' she says. 'my name is molly.'

chapter eleven

I hug her harder against me, terrified she'll fade away like a good dream.

We eventually break apart, and it's like peeling flesh from bone.

"That help?" Molly asks.

"More than you can imagine."

"What now?"

"Let's get out of here."

"Home?"

"Yes." I nod, wrapping my arm around her shoulder and pulling her close against me as we walk toward the open street. "Uh, where is that again?"

She looks up at me, concerned. "Jesus, what happened to you?"

"Well . . . "

All words escape me as my breath retreats in my gut, legs going stiff and refusing to budge another inch. My aroused penis shrivels. A bubble of air gets caught in the middle of my throat, and if I wasn't so preoccupied with what I see ahead of me, I'd probably be choking right now.

There, across the street, watching me.

Bio mask strapped around its mouth, a white apron tied to its torso, a large cooler held in its grim little hand. I don't think I have to guess what is inside. Despite our distance, I can still feel the creature smelling me from afar, breathing in my own dismal aura.

I try to work my mind powers on it again,

concentrating on another spidery explosion, but come up empty.

Then a crowd of drunks stumble in front of us, and by the time they pass the gloomy surgeon is nowhere in sight. I do a quick scan around the perimeter without moving from where I'm standing, but it's vanished.

"Bobby? Are you all right?" Molly asks, waving her hand in front of my face. "What's wrong?"

I take a deep breath. "I'll tell you about it on the way."

It is a fifteen-minute walk, and another ten minutes before I am able to accept that I've really found my home and it isn't all some dream.

It's in an apartment building, three stories up, the seventh door on the left. I'm sure to most, walking in their building and trudging up the steps to their door must seem like just some other tedious task they have to deal with, but to me, right now, it is quite the opposite. It's one of the most spiritual moments I've experienced all night, and that's saying a lot.

There's only three rooms in the apartment. Upon walking through the front door, I'm met with a brief hallway. A kitchen sprouts off to the left, but if I keep moving forward I soon enter a large bedroom. Against the left wall of this room there is a door leading to a bathroom. Back in the bedroom, I find the bare essentials: mattress on the floor, a dresser, dirty clothes piled around it, a little TV resting on a cardboard box beside the mattress.

Against one of the walls stands a wooden contraption with four legs, a small mattress placed inside its wide opening. I know what it is right away, and what it is for. This is where a baby sleeps.

Around the crib, I see numerous diapers, outfits too tiny to fit any of us, and a pile of shiny toys that I am very tempted to play with. However, what I *don't* see is an actual baby.

"Hey, you gonna shower?" Molly asks, heading into the kitchen.

"What?"

"You're filthy. You should go wash up or something."

"Oh, um, right."

"You hungry? I can make something if you want."

"Yes, please." My stomach grumbles in agreement.

"Okay, well go on and take a shower and when you get out, it should be ready. Love you, hon."

Without any strain, the words leave my mouth as naturally as air enters my lungs: "I love you, too."

I start to head for the bathroom but stop myself. I'll need clothes first, won't I? Yes. I turn in the other direction and approach the dresser, shuffling through the unfolded mess until I find what I need: a pair of jeans, underwear, and a black T-shirt.

I go into the bathroom and close the door behind me, laying the clothes on the sink and hanging my trench coat up behind the door before stepping into the shower. It isn't a very complex system, and before long I've managed to turn the hot water on.

The water showering all of the dirt away, I close my eyes and enjoy the warmth and safety it provides. This is what I've been blindly searching for all night. Home. This is home. I am home.

But for how long?

Surely Lamb's goons know where I live. Whoever Lamb works for is going to be pissed that I killed one of his right-hand men. How long will it take before they come barging in through the front door, pumping me and Molly both full of lead? We won't stand a chance, hiding up here.

After I've showered and dressed, I find Molly sitting on the mattress with a bowl of food in her lap, watching the television with another untouched bowl balancing beside her on a pillow. She has changed into a pair of sweatpants and a purple V-Neck T-shirt.

Sinking my weight on the mattress, I crawl up close to

her and grab the bowl off the pillow. I grab the fork sticking out of it and twirl a pile of noodles into my mouth. There isn't much flavor to it, but it satisfies my hunger. On the television we watch some cartoon, the characters indistinguishable from each other.

"Feel better?" Molly asks.

"Yeah, I do, actually."

"Good. How's the food?"

"It's good."

"Okay, now I know things have seriously changed," Molly says, tossing her fork back in the bowl, disgusted. "This shit is *horrible*."

I shrug. "It's okay."

"My ass."

"That is okay, too."

She snorts. "Are you saying that my ass is of equal worth to a bowl of shitty Ramen noodles?"

What the hell is she talking about? "I do not particularly care for where this conversation is heading. You seem a little upset."

"Yeah, well, your dick is just as good as cottage cheese."

"You've just insulted me, yes?"

"I don't know," she says. "Depends on if you like cottage cheese or not, I guess."

"Do I?"

"No one likes cottage cheese."

"Oh."

I try to think of a good comeback but my mind seems to be too busy conjuring up an image of a big ass trapped in a bowl of noodles. It is surprisingly disturbing.

We watch more cartoons, finishing up our food, and Molly takes both our bowls in the kitchen.

"Do we have a kid?" I ask, once she returns.

She looks at me, a little taken back, but seems to remember my unfortunate situation. "Er, yeah, we do. We have a daughter. Her name is Ezzy. She just turned two a couple of weeks ago."

"Oh, okay, cool."

And it is pretty cool. I like the feeling, knowing that I have a daughter. I wonder if she shares her mother's eyes. Those magnificent green eyes . . .

"You really didn't know, huh?"

"I guess not," I reply sadly.

"I was almost sure you would have. I just thought . . . ya know? You two are so close."

"Yeah?"

"Yeah."

"That's good, thank you. Makes me happy to hear." Then I add, "Do I have any other family? Parents? Siblings?"

She shakes her head. "Your parents died before we met. And you were a single child, so no."

"Oh." I clear my throat. "So, um, where is Ezzy now?"

"Babysitter's. He'll drop her off in a few hours. I'm technically supposed to still be at work. Although, I'm not so sure I even have a job anymore. And, judging by the sound of things, neither do you. So this probably doesn't leave us in the best situation."

"I'm sorry. I don't' know how, exactly, but this is all my fault."

Molly kisses me on the cheek, my stubble tickling her face. "I'm just glad you're okay, after all you've been through tonight."

"It still isn't over, though, whatever it is—not by a long shot," I say. "Do you have any idea what this could all be about?"

Molly shakes her head, frowning. "Sorry, honey, but you refused to tell me anything about your work. You said it was for my own safety. In fact, your meeting with Lamb tonight is the most you've ever revealed about it the entire length of our relationship."

"And how long has that been?"

"Well, let's see, a little over five years now," Molly says. "You were twenty-four when we met, and I was twenty-seven, so . . . yeah, it fits."

"You're *thirty-two?*"

She sniggers. "You're not so far behind yourself, slick."

"Yeah, well, I know, but . . . damn, *really?* You don't look any older than, like, well, you don't look thirty-two is what I am trying to say here. Not at all."

She blushes, so I figure I must have said something good. "You are too cute sometimes. Especially when you've lost your memory."

"Uh, thanks."

"Shut up and kiss me," she says, eyeing me under seductive lashes.

"Okay," I say, and I do.

We kiss for what feels like hours, our hands roaming our bodies and gradually stripping ourselves as our passion intensifies.

(*somewhere in another lifetime, back when i'm still twenty-four and she's still twenty-seven, my lips are upon her, the atmosphere growing warmer despite our progressive lack of clothing. our kiss deepens.*)

I roll her over on her back, the rowdy cartoon characters on TV now nothing more than forgotten background music. Our lips never part, even as I slide myself inside of her. Despite my condition, it all comes so naturally. This is right.

(*it couldn't be more perfect, i'm thinking, as she wraps her bare legs around my waist and pushes me closer against her, so close that we are no longer two separate beings but one connected entity.*)

I hear her gasp as I rock against her, her breath heavy on my neck. All the frustration and mystery of the night fades and all I can concentrate on is the spiritual ball of rising heat and knowledge building up between us. It is now that I am certain not everything is completely screwed, after all. No, there is still good in this world and I believe I am living it right now. I am creating it. We both are.

(*our breaths become heavy and more rapid as her*

nails claw into my back, scratching my flesh. it is a pain that does not hurt, but is welcomed. it is a fuel that makes our hypnotic rhythm increase with speed, completely losing ourselves in a cloud of perfection, an angel's moan caressing the ceiling above us.)

And together we let ourselves go, melting into each other as if all physical form has evolved to something more philosophical. I collapse down on her, arms still bound around her like glue, not wanting the moment to ever end, determined to stay like this forever, eternally swimming together in our own mutual zenith.

(even after it is over, my grip refuses to loosen from around her, fearing she'll drift away from me like mist. i don't know how i've found her but i sure as hell know i will never be the same if i were to lose her now that i have her. tonight will always last, i think, five years ago. i'll be living this night every night for the rest of my life and as long as it stays this way, everything will be fine. so let it stay.)

This is how you remember.

You relive.

ii.

a night to co-exist

chapter twelve

I wake up with Molly in my arms, her head resting on my chest, gently surfing with the waves of my lungs breathing in and out.

There are no corpses here.

Born into hell and delivered to heaven.

I wish I could stay like this forever, but the rising urge to urinate grows too strong. I crawl out of bed, replacing my body with a pillow for Molly to cuddle. She doesn't seem to notice a difference. It confirms how essential my existence is when I can easily be replaced with a sack of feathers and fluff.

Well, at least I know one thing that pillow can't do that I can . . .

An image flashes in my head, contradicting what I had just thought. Needing to clarify something, my legs force themselves over to the dresser and I pull open the top drawer, rifling through it until I discover the object in my thoughts.

A small, metallic egg shape contraption that I automatically register as the pillow equivalent of my penis.

('*what the hell is this?*'

'*oh, that's BOB.*'

'*what?*'

'*haha, my battery-operated buddy. you know, BOB.*'

'*um.*'

'*heh, that's funny. i never put you two together before until now. what do you suppose it means?*'

'um.'

'hey, i know, you could be my big bob and that can be my little BOB! or, well, i guess it could be the other way around, too, depending on the weather.')

"Oh, son of a bitch," I mutter under my breath, studying its terrifying features. *I don't trust you,* I tell it, and toss it on top of the dresser.

I sigh and turn around, heading into the bathroom to relieve myself. I flush and dig out the bottle of ibuprofen from my coat pocket hanging behind the door, dry swallowing three of the tablets.

Molly has woken by the time I return to bed. She sits up, rubbing her eyes. I sit down beside her, one arm curling around her waist and massaging her lower back.

She yawns. "What time is it?"

"No idea."

"How long have I been sleeping?"

"A couple of days."

"What?"

"I don't know. Not very long."

"Ezzy should've been home by now," she says.

"Is her being late . . . unusual? Should we be concerned?"

"They probably got caught up playing some game. I'm sure it's fine."

My lips curl into a smile at the thought of my child. "I can't wait to meet her. Uh, again."

She touches my cheek and strokes my facial hair, saying, "You two will kick it off with no problem. Don't worry about it." Her face changes, eyes widening and jaw dropping, as her hand moves from my cheek to behind my head. "Jesus, what happened to your neck?"

"What do you mean?"

Her finger lightly brushes across it and I flinch, squealing out in pain. Sure enough, the headache has now returned with a vengeance, grinding its hellish fangs deep into my brain. "Don't touch whatever you just touched again!"

"Sorry, just it's all bruised looking," Molly says, retracting her hand.

"Yeah, well, a lot of my body is pretty bruised up tonight in case you haven't noticed."

"No, I know, but this is different. It's, like, black, or something . . . like it's infected. Oh my god, no wonder it hurts . . . "

"How bad does it look?"

"There's something in the dead center of it all, like an opened scab, or something. It looks like you were shot. Holy crap."

"I think if I had been shot in my neck I would be dead right now."

"Yeah, no shit, slick," Molly says. "I just said that's what it looks like, is all."

"Is there any blood in it? What does it look like?"

"I already told you," Molly says, craning her neck back for a closer inspection. "It's like this deep hole, but I don't see any blood. It's like this black crust."

"Mud?"

'I don't think so. This stuff looks more . . . " She trails off, leaving me waiting.

"More *what*?"

"More evil."

That is a word I never *ever* want to hear someone use to describe something on my body.

Evil?

What the fuck?

A loud series of bangs erupt at the front door. We both jump.

"Who the hell is that?" I whisper.

"Oh, probably just the Rev dropping off Ezzy. I told you they'd be here sooner or later."

She gets out of bed and redresses in her sweats and purple V-Neck, striding across the living room to the front door. Still on my guard, I slide into my jeans and underwear, but before I have a chance to find my T-shirt, someone screams at the front door.

Molly.

Shit.

She stumbles backward into the living room, collapsing on her ass. Two men—one I recognize as Raoul—barge in, slamming the door behind them. They are both packing submachine guns, and neither one of them look like they are in the mood to screw around. Raoul particularly, who grips his weapon with one hand only, the other hand now bandaged in layers of bloodstained gauze. The same type of gauze is applied to his shoulder, as well.

"No one fucking move!" he yells, waving his gun.

"Whoa, whoa, fellas." I hold my hands up. "Can we help you with something?"

"Yeah, you can help me by saying one more word, because as soon as you do, I will gladly tear your face to pieces with this here gun. So come on. Say it. Just one word, motherfucker. That's all I need."

Raoul looks at the other goon. "I told you we should have just came here first. You know how much time we would have saved?"

"I'm sorry, I just didn't think someone would be stupid enough to hide out at their home when they know people are out to kill them. Especially people who know where they live . . . "

Raoul sniggers, as if he's been waiting for him to say that. "Well, you see, Trig, normally your assumption would have been correct, but the thing is, Bob here isn't exactly the smartest of the bunch." He glances over at me. "Isn't that right?"

I offer a guilty smile, as if to say, "You caught me."

"Not to mention the fact that lately he seems to be having some problems with the ol' memory box," Raoul adds. "But that's okay, he isn't gonna be around long enough to have time to remember anything. All he needs to know is that he's living on stolen time as it is. Indigo wants his head on a motherfucking platter. You got all that, Bob?"

I nod.

"Now, since you've recently been suffering some brain damage, I am sure you're expecting me to kill you right here and now—and believe me, I would *love* that more than anything else, but it is not meant to be. You and your pretty little girlfriend are gonna go on a trip with us back to the casino, and Indigo will properly deal with you. But don't get the wrong idea, I have full permission to make your face go away with bullets if you so much as breathe funny. I *will* kill you. Kill you to *death*."

No shit, I think, but only nod in acknowledgement.

"Another thing, I know you got a piece hiding somewhere here," Raoul says, gesturing to his shoulder. Then something seems to click in his mind, so he says, "Oh, and speaking of which . . . "

He calmly walks over to me, sporting one hell of a grin, and without another word kicks me square in the testicles. Molly screams. I double over and collapse on my stomach, gasping for air.

"Shut up, bitch," the other man, Trig, says.

Raoul crouches next to me and whispers, "We're not even close to being even, baby. I don't know how you did what you did to my hand, but I will make you pay before we get to the casino. You and your whore."

"We'll see about that," I say.

He laughs. "Yeah, you'll see, all right. So, you gonna tell me where this gun is or am I gonna have to start chopping off Molly's tits?"

He delivers a swift chop to the throat, creating a temporary block in my airways and making me choke on a breath inhaled prematurely. Both hands shoot up at my neck, my mouth wide open and gagging for clean air. I can't make up my mind over which to hold: my throat or my scrotum.

Molly screams again and Raoul tells Trig to shut her the fuck up. He obeys, casually walking over to her, and backhands her across the face. *Hard.* She yelps like a puppy getting its tail stepped on and flies back against the wall, smacking against the plaster and falling silent.

Still crouched next to me, Raoul says, in a near growl, "Where. Is. The. Gun."

There's no use resisting, I know this now, not when Molly's health is on the line. She is the only one I know in this world, the only one who makes me feel at home. I need her by my side or else everything will crumble, everything will die.

Ashamed, I point in the direction of the bathroom, refusing to look him in the eyes.

"What, in the bathroom?" Raoul asks. "The gun's in there?"

I nod.

"Where at?"

"Co—*ooot*," I stammer, choking again. It feels as if someone has tied a rope around my throat. It won't be much longer before my windpipe is completely crushed and I topple over, defeated at last.

"Say that one more time?" Raoul leans close to my ear and if my balls weren't halfway up my stomach, I might've mustered up the courage to headbutt this fucker.

"Coat... it's ... *craa* ... *ah* ... coat. Pock ... *craa* ... et!"

"Coat pocket?" he asks.

I nod, gagging on phlegm.

"Don't take your eyes away from these two for a second," Raoul tells Trig. "Slightest bit of trouble, don't hesitate to shoot. Do away with the girl first, then him. I want him to see with his own eyes what happens when you disobey me."

"No prob," Trig says, tapping the submachine gun in his hands. "It's been too long since I've killed someone, anyway. Starting to get rusty."

Raoul heads into the bathroom and searches for the coat, pulling back the shower curtain and coming up empty. After a second or two he finally figures it out, spotting it behind the door, and closes it to allow him better access, no doubt ransacking through the pockets in search of the weapon.

Like I would really be stupid enough to leave the gun in the bathroom.

I glance across the room at the mattress, trying to engage my x-ray vision but failing. It's okay. I know what's under there, awaiting my touch. All I need to do is make it over there, pull it out from under the mattress, turn around, and shoot the two goons before they shoot me.

Or I can make their heads explode. Just focus hard enough and make them both go *pop*.

How long have I had this power, anyway? This isn't natural. It's beyond fucked up.

But it's coming in handy.

I stare at Trig and concentrate. I imagine his brain exploding within his skull and turning his entire head to mush. I think about the way his body will drop once there's nothing on top of his shoulders.

Die, you bastard, die . . .

"Your girl isn't looking so good, bro," Trig says, unfazed by my attempts. "I think I might have hit her too hard. Damn, good thing boss only cares about you, huh?"

He steps toward Molly.

"Oh, shit," he says, and calls out, "Dude, Raoul, I think I fuckin' killed this broad."

"I don't care," Raoul replies from behind the door. "All I've found so far is a candy bar. Why are there so many damn *pockets* in this thing?"

Trig approaches Molly lying limp against the wall. He's so close that his back is now turned against me, confirming that he was right, he *is* rusty. Then I start worrying about Molly's state of health and an intense wave of anger overpowers everything.

What the fuck did he do?

The window next to Trig explodes and he screams, backing away and holding his hands up to his face. He turns toward me, revealing a face full of glass.

I jump up and scan the area for any potential weapons. Despite the glass, he still hasn't dropped his submachine gun. I pick up the first solid hard object I come across without even paying attention to what it is. It's heavy and feels like it can get the job done and this is all that matters right now.

Even if it is my girlfriend's vibrator.

I make it barely three feet before I stop dead in my tracks, frozen as Trig's submachine gun pushes into my face. He grins, blood dripping down his face. "Nice try, fuckface."

His grin is short-lived, replaced by another scream and choking sound as his windpipes crush without me touching him. He drops the submachine gun and falls to the floor, hands around his neck, gagging. I stare at him and continue concentrating on his throat. He's falling apart. I'm killing a man by my thoughts. I am unstoppable. I am God.

I am dangerous.

Holy shitballs.

Gunfire bursts from the bathroom doorway. I dive to the ground as a spray of bullets sink into the wall behind me, and I can't help but wonder if I'd still be alive if Raoul hadn't lost all function with his good hand earlier.

Still on the ground, I throw the vibrator toward Raoul. It bashes against his nose, knocking him back into the bathroom. I'm on my feet and sprinting toward him before he has a chance to recover his firearm. I punch him repeatedly and scream, telling him he fucked with the wrong person, telling him that I won't stop until him and every one of his piece of shit goons are dead.

I punch him a few more times, but it's useless. The guy's done. He stares up at me with eyes devoid of life.

Behind me, Molly screams my name, and a gunshot rings out. I spin around just in time to see Trig drop to the floor, blood and brains gushing out of his skull. Molly stands across the room, gripping the gun I'd found at the river. She shakes and cries and drops it at her feet. I meet her halfway in the room and hug her.

"Holy shit, Bobby," she says. "I killed a guy."

"It gets easier," I tell her, and I know it's the wrong thing to say, but I still say it, anyway. Sometimes there is no right thing to say.

All these killings. All these bodies.

All this blood.

None of this is about what I've become.

It's about what I've always been.

"Jesus fucking Christ," I whisper, or maybe I shout it, who can say right now? I'm breaking down. Body shaking. Lips quivering. "What did I do? What have I done? I fucking . . . I've killed. I killed people. I fucking killed people." My legs nearly lose their balance. They feel like rubber. I wrap my arms around Molly's back and latch on with a fierce grip, rambling lunatic sobs. "What am I?" I ask, begging for an answer, any answer, the eyes of those I killed looking at me, pleading for their lives to be returned. *"What am I?"*

Molly manages to loosen herself from my kung fu grip just enough to find the leverage to kiss me on the forehead. I feel like such a miserable embarrassment crying like this in front of her but I can't help it, it just keeps coming and coming and oh my god my balls really do hurt. I'm a merciless murderer and my throat is sore and my balls feel like they've been squashed up to my stomach.

Her soothing lips depart from skin ever so slightly, and she whispers, "You are the love of my life, Bobby. You're not a killer. You were *protecting* me. You are a good man, do you understand that? I don't know the details of your work but I'm sure it isn't as bad as the mystery implies. And besides, whatever it is, it helped feed our daughter. The beautiful, perfect child who you and I created. Together. So please, get a hold of yourself, there is nothing wrong with you except for the fact that you're having trouble remembering what a terrific family you belong to.

And now that we are together again, there is no reason to fear. I love you, Bobby, and you love me, and that is all there is to it. Got it?"

I push my hungry mouth forward, inhaling her again, knowing she is exactly what I need. I wonder what would have happened had I chosen to go down a different path other than the one leading to The Risqué Cabaret. Would I already be dead?

I kiss her deeper and try to forget that I've forgotten.

chapter thirteen

While Molly packs clothes into a duffle bag, I wander off into the kitchen to wash the blood off my chest. I scrub myself with an old sponge. Old food and mold scrape against my flesh. It's preferable to brain matter.

Maybe Molly's right. I was just protecting her. I'm not a killer. I'm a good man.

No. I know who I am. What I am.

What truth do I fear? That I'm a cold-blooded murderer—a *monster*? Maybe I'm better off buying into Molly's spin of who I am, of what makes me *me*.

Bob.

Big Bob.

Brother Bob.

Who are you, you bastard?

Obviously Bob isn't my real name. I reminiscence back to my little hallway interlude, when me and my other self finally got our turn with the man behind the desk, picking out new names for the people in line.

Picking out new names.

Earlier in the apartment, I'd told Molly about the flashback, but she didn't seem to fully connect the meaning. Does she realize Bob isn't my real name? Does she know, that for some reason, I've been lying to her all this time?

The question is—*why?* What do I have to hide?

And of course, the answer is obvious.

Monster.

"Babe, you almost ready to go?"

"Yeah," I call out, squeezing a stream of pink water out of the sponge and watching it splash into the metal basin below, "give me a minute."

One day we will all splash down the faucet, and into the river we will go.

I sigh, dropping the bloody sponge into the basin. I debate emptying my gun into my own skull—wipe all this misery out in one quick, painless bang. It's almost frightening, how powerful the temptation is.

Then I hear Molly's voice again, calling my name. Her voice makes the entertainment of suicide ludicrous.

I bend over the refrigerator, scavenging through the sparse contents inside: a couple cans of soda pop, a slice of cheese, some lunchmeat, a half-eaten hamburger wrapped in foil, and a full bottle of milk. I quickly devour the hamburger, overwhelmed by an unexpected hunger, and grimace at its bitter cold taste. Two seconds after tossing the last bite in my mouth is when, of course, I spot the microwave plugged in on top of the fridge.

The fridge's frost chills over my flesh as I hug the bottle of milk and head back into the living room, finding Molly sitting down on the mattress, watching cartoons. The packed duffle bag rests on the ground beside her. I unzip the bag, revealing clothes, diapers, and baby toys. I stuff the cola and bottle inside and close it again.

"You all set to go then?" I ask.

"Yup," she says, not taking her eyes off the television set.

I grab a T-shirt from the floor and pull it over me, scanning the room for any available footwear.

"Hey, uh, Mol?" I say, and a wonderful feeling soothes through my body as soon as I call her by her shortened down name. Mol . . . this is what I've always called her. It's so natural, I could die comfortably.

"Yeah, babe?" Molly says.

"Do I have any shoes around here?"

"Um, you would have had them on your feet when you left for work today, so . . . "

"Yeah, I'm thinking those shoes are probably in the same place as the rest of the clothes I was wearing today."

"And those are . . . where, again?"

I give her an incredulous look.

"Oh, right. Duh."

"So I don't own any other shoes? Not one single other pair to my name?"

"Well, you have those rabbit slippers. What did you call them? Your funny bunnies?"

I sigh, looking around for the slippers. Molly giggles behind me.

"What's so funny?" I ask, feigning irritation. In reality, the sound of her laughter is like heaven on earth.

I turn around just in time to see her pointing at the television set, her other hand covering up her mouth to suppress the disruptive fit of giggles.

"They . . . they . . . they painted the dog *pink!*" Molly shouts, completely losing it. At first, I find it baffling that she could be watching cartoons right now. There are literal dead men in the same room. But what's the alternative? What else is she supposed to be doing? This is as good of an escape as any.

"I love you," I tell her.

Then the front door opens and I hear a man saying, "The hell . . . "

I waste no time in picking up Little BOB from the floor and hurling it across the room toward the general direction of the voice. A man with crazy, spiked blue hair ducks and drops to the ground just as the vibrator flies over his head.

"What the hell was that?" he yells. "A grenade?"

"No, it was a vibrator! And there's plenty more where that came from!"

Molly gasps behind me. "You found my Jack Rabbit, too?"

I pick up the submachine gun lying next to Trig's

corpse and point it at the spiky-haired punk. He doesn't look to be a threat, but I still can't afford to let my guard down.

"You one of Lamb's boys, huh?" I yell at him. "You see what I did to the last pack of rats he sent along?" I gesture to Trig.

Instead of becoming dreadfully frightened as I had imagined, the man starts to laugh. "Look at you, all serious and shit. Oh, who's a menacing wee boy? You are! You are!"

"Excuse me?"

"Bobby, relax," Molly says from behind me. "It's just the Rev."

"The what?"

"The Rev. He's Ezzy's babysitter."

"Oh."

I lower the submachine gun, offering a guilty smile.

He raises his eyebrow at me. "Having problems there, are we, mate?"

I know who this guy is. I've seen him before. Tonight, actually. But at the same time, it was also over five years ago. He had been younger, just like myself back then.

Back then, his hair had been green.

"Where is my daughter?" I ask.

"Oh, um . . . " He clears his throat and, in a low, barely audible tone, says, "In the dumpster."

"*What?*"

Looking at his feet, the Rev repeats himself. "The . . . dumpster?"

This time it is Molly who says it. "*What?*"

"The dumpster!" he shouts. "Goddamn, are you blokes deaf or what?"

"*What?*" On that particular "what" it happens to be Molly and I both.

"The dump—"

"Why the fuck is she in the dumpster?" I demand. Molly is already running out the door, down the hallway. The Rev and I follow her lead in a jog.

As we hit the stairs, he tries to explain. "Well shit, mate, I walk up to the building and suddenly I hear all this shooting. I didn't know what the hell was going on. Me figures, some blokes with guns are gonna be coming out, you know, fleeing the scene, and I had the baby with me just standing there like some wanker. So I stashed her in the dumpster to be on the safe side. After a while, when no one came out, I decided to come up and check to see if the coast was clear. Apparently it is. And apparently you also turned into some kind of badass Rambo boy overnight."

We make it down the steps and Molly's already outside, running across the street and into an alleyway. She struggles to climb the dumpster, her perfect little legs kicking back and forth to initiate progress. By the time we join her in the alley Molly has already managed to fall inside the dumpster, sobbing in what I take to be relief.

I'm out of breath and my bare feet ache from running across gravel, but none of that seems to matter. Molly stands up in the dumpster with a child cradled in her arms.

I instinctively think of her as *our* child, and I suddenly have the urge to punch the spiky-haired punk square in the face for what he has done with her. What he has done with *my* child. Then a more sensible part of me tries to convince myself that what he did is exactly what he should have done. This is probably the safest place he could have hidden her. Whoever this guy is, he is okay. I think he's a friend—*my* friend. And he must be, if I trust him enough to babysit my own daughter.

I glance over at the Rev, also trying to catch his breath, and give him a nod in approval, as if to say, "Thank you for stashing my baby in a dumpster."

He nods back. "You're welcome."

Her panting subsiding, tears rolling down her cheeks, Molly showers our baby with a series of kisses all over her face and then hands her to me so she can climb out of the dumpster. Hesitant, I reach out and take the baby (*my baby*) in my arms, anxiety fading as soon as she settles into a comfortable position. She's the last piece to an extensive jigsaw puzzle connecting everything in the universe together at once.

She is so small, so fragile. Her entire life depends on me. All I have to do is squeeze hard enough and bam, she's gone. I have control. Looking down at her, she looks back up at me, and I think she understands this. I think she understands this better than myself.

I thought Molly was the most beautiful thing I would ever lay my eyes upon tonight, or any other night, but I was wrong. I hadn't thought about what kind of beauty the both of us would be able to create together.

Even if someone had told me previously, I don't think I would have believed them. She . . . this creation in my arms, this gift . . . she is unreal. Not of this world.

The rapid beat in my heart ceases, going on an indefinite hiatus as I try to comprehend the sheer amount of power and certainty that this tiny being delivers into my soul. Every detail sinks into my consciousness at once. Her dark, curly brown hair. Her round, beautiful face. Rosy cheeks. Her small, delicate hands. Fingers gripping the fabric of my T-shirt. A red and black checkered kilt strapped around her waist, the hems ending at her ankles. The baby blue T-shirt with the words MY MOM'S TITS ARE BIGGER THAN YOURS printed across the chest.

But none of these are the most important detail. Incredible, yes—but not the detail I train all of my focus on. I look deep into her eyes, the eyes that match her mother's. So green they're almost uncanny. They are just how I imagined. Perfect. She is perfect. So, so perfect. She is mine. My own.

My baby girl.

(interlude iii)

me #2 paces back and forth, shoes squeaking on the waxed linoleum each time he turns around, hands frantically running through his wild black hair, making it stand up all over the place. and judging from the look on his face, his mind is probably somewhere in the same general area.

i find myself sitting at the edge of a sink, arms crossed, just watching me #2 go crazy. and surprise, surprise, we're in a public bathroom again. there's a whole row of sinks next to me, the one i'm sitting on being the last one in line, a square mirror above each of them. nothing strange here—minus the hysterical man in the dead center of the room, of course. his eyes are watered up and he keeps breathing heavily, in and out, in and out, like he's hyperventilating.

'fuck!' me #2 shouts, punching his thigh and marching over to the sink i'm resting on. he places a hand on either side of it for support and leans forward, staring straight into my eyes.

for a second i almost believe he's looking at me rather than the mirror. but i know i'm not really here—at least not in the literal sense. although, in a way, i guess i am. i once was here, and now i am reliving it.

but as what? a ghost?

'you fucking idiot,' me #2 says into my face. 'you're just a lie, a goddamn lie. too close, you got too close, too . . . too close. just a lie and another lie. can't . . . lies. shit.

shit. shit. this is fucked. this is so fucked. what did he say, you fucking idiot? now what? what happens later?'

he stops talking, just stares at himself for a while through the mirror, through myself. after so long he finally gains control of his breathing and he turns on the sink, splashing some water in his face until the door opens and a man with a long green mohawk hurries inside.

'bobby, man, what the fuck are you doing, huh?' he asks. 'you missed it.'

speaking in a very calm and levelheaded voice, me #2 says, 'it's over already?'

'yeah, it's done. you got mol scared, mate. what's going on?'

'i don't know. i guess i freaked out. this is all just . . . you know?'

'yeah, i understand. no worries, huh? come on. let's go check out your little girl.'

'how . . . how is she?' me #2 asks.

the rev sighs, glancing over at the wall. 'bobby, i don't know how to break this to you, so i'll just tell you straight out. your daughter . . . she only has eight fingers.'

'what?'

'but, on the plus side, she also has two thumbs.'

'i am going to kill you.'

'nah, save that for later. right now you have something more important to deal with.'

'yeah, you're right. but don't think i'm gonna forget about that.'

'you will, too, and you know it,' the rev says as they start to exit the bathroom. i try to follow them but a strange shield forces me to stay where i am on the sink.

'okay, that may be true,' i hear me #2 saying. 'but sometime in the future, like two or three years from now, i am totally gonna remember. then i'll kill you.'

'fair enough,' the rev says, and then they are both gone, the bathroom door swinging shut behind them.

'well, now what?' i ask the empty room, my words

nothing more than surreal sound waves drifting among the air.

it answers me by dragging my nonexistent body backwards, pulling me over the sink and into the mirror. but instead of shattering the glass like my reflexes expect, i dissolve into the material like it's a thick goo.

i try to scream but it is no use. before i can so much as open my nonexistent mouth, my entire body is drowning in this sea of mirrors, everything twirling around and around until i find myself clawing out the other side, out of another mirror.

caught in a frenzied whirlwind, i drop onto the floor with an imagined thud. i've been sent to a small hospital room. a woman with long red hair lies covered on a bed in front of me, rocking a baby in her arms.

the door swings open and in comes good ol' brother bob, marching in this numb trance toward the bed, his hands shaking at his waist.

'oh god, molly, i'm so sorry . . .'

her head shoots up, worry written across her face. 'what happened?'

me #2 collapses down on his knees next to the bed, his elbows pushing into the cushion.

'i'm sorry, it was just all . . . it was all too much. i panicked. i'm here now, okay? and i'm never leaving again. i'm here, i'm here, i'm here . . .'

'that's right, you are here,' molly says. 'and that's all that matters.'

'yes.'

'now, would you like to hold our baby?'

i can damn near feel me #2's heartbeat pounding against his chest at the thought of holding her.

smiling, molly hands over the baby and me #2 cradles her in his arms, ever so gently, fearing he'll break her in half with the slightest pressure. i know this is what he is afraid of at the moment because this is what i'm afraid of, too.

we both look down at our newborn baby, at her eyes, her beautiful, green eyes. and i know we're thinking the same thing. she couldn't be more perfect. fuck everything else. it'll eventually figure itself out. everything is going to be fine. yes. it is okay.

and it always will be okay as long as our family is together. our beloved other half—yes, that is the correct term for what molly is, i realize now. she is our other half. and this wonderful creation in our arms . . . she, she is the key who locks both halves into place for all of eternity.

our baby girl.

chapter fourteen

"Da-doo."

I fall back into reality, standing next to a dumpster with my little girl gently cradled in my arms, her perfect green eyes staring up at me and projecting all the beautiful secrets of humanity.

"Da-doo!"

God, her voice is every bit as wonderful as the rest of her. I just want to hold her and squeeze her against my chest like this and never let go.

"Yes, baby?"

"Hi!" my baby girl (*Ezzy . . . her name is Ezzy*) shouts.

"Hi!" I shout back, just as excited to see her as she apparently is to see me.

Off in some other world, Molly manages to climb out of the dumpster, brushing sticky globs of garbage off her clothing in disgust.

"Eww!" Ezzy laughs, using her tiny thumb and index finger to squeeze her nostrils together. "Yuck!"

"Yeah, honey, yuck is the right word," Molly says, flinging what appears to be a used condom over in the Rev's direction. Unfortunately her aim is just a little off and it goes *SPLAT!* against the bricked wall behind him.

The Rev flinches back, as if he's expecting another round of condom attacks, and says, "Eh, the hell? That was unsanitary as shit."

"And leaving my child in a dumpster wasn't?" Molly asks.

"Oh, you'd rather I took her upstairs to the fookin' gun show, yeah? Come off it, Mol. And besides, it's not like I threw a splooge balloon at her or anything. Really, that was just uncalled for."

Molly sighs and grabs Ezzy from me, pressing her head against her shoulder. I am stricken with the urge to take her back and yell MINE! but somehow at the last second I am able to stop myself. "All right, you may have a point. But I'm still upset with you."

The Rev offers a white flag of laughter as we all head out of the alley. "Yeah, when aren't you? Hell, last week you were pissed at me 'cause I brought Bob-O home with a tat of Betty Boop on his ass."

I stop walking. "Wait, I have a tattoo on my ass?"

"Betty Boop is a whore," Molly says.

"Whore!" Ezzy echoes.

Not wanting Ezzy to see the dead bodies up in our apartment, we have the Rev stay outside with her on the sidewalk while Molly and I go back up to retrieve the duffle bag, along with her shoes and my . . . uh, slippers. I make sure to stash one of the submachine guns in my trench coat's large pockets for safe keeping. This thing is long from over. A part of me feels like it never will end.

When we return outside, the Rev gives my funny bunnies one look and nods in approval. "Right on."

"Thanks." I shuffle the duffle bag between arms, charging up my strength.

"Well, now what?" Molly asks, holding Ezzy close to her chest. Her eyes are closed and she couldn't look more at peace with the world.

"I guess you lot could start by filling me in on what wonderful adventure I seem to have missed out on."

"We need to get moving first," I say. "It isn't safe here anymore. How far away is your place?"

He looks at me like I must be joking. It is a look I've become familiar with tonight. "Nice one, mate."

"It isn't too far, Bobby," Molly says. "C'mon, let's go."

We head down the sidewalk, the Rev stumbling behind us, trying to make sense of the situation. "Bob, I don't mean to point out the obvious, but you aren't well tonight, are you?"

"What was your first clue?"

"Well, uh, probably the dead dude up in your apartment."

"*Two* dead dudes."

"Oh, shit. Okay, then the *two* dead dudes up in your apartment. Yeah, that was my first clue. But, uh, you see mate, you got some black shit all over your neck there."

"Yeah, so I've heard."

"Man, what the hell is that? Now I *know* that shit isn't sanitary. Not at all."

"No, I suppose it isn't."

"So are any of you blokes gonna tell me what the hell is going on or what?" the Rev asks.

"You really want to hear it?"

"No, I don't want to hear anything about how you straight up murdered a motherfucker. What do you think?"

When I'm finished, the only question he has for me is why I felt the need to go into detail during my and Molly's sex scene.

"Just because," I tell him. "Just because."

I don't know how it's possible but the Rev's place is even shittier than my own apartment. What he lives in barely qualifies as an apartment. A motel room wouldn't do the place justice. The word "garage" comes to mind, yet that isn't exactly right, either. It's this big open space with a stone floor, four walls, and a heavy titanium door that we have to push up to get inside. There are a dozen identical garages lined up next to each other—whether other people live in these, I have no idea. To be honest, I'm a little shocked that the Rev lives here. But he does. At least *someone* does—the half-broken futon and the myriad piles of discarded clothing make enough of a case.

We pull the door down, hiding us from the outside world. There is no way to lock it from the inside, so any real safety is more imagined than factual. The Rev pulls a long chain down from the center of the ceiling and a dim light bulb brightens next to it. For the moment, we have escaped the darkness. Although I know it is not far behind.

Ezzy scrambles in Molly's grasp until she sets her down on the floor. She crawls over to the futon and snatches up a purple teddy bear, hugging it close to her soft chest.

"Oh, shit, didn't even realize I had forgotten that," the Rev said. He bends over a small refrigerator plugged into the corner of the room and grabs three bottles of beer out of it, giving one to myself and one to Molly.

"You know damn well we would have never gotten her to sleep tonight if she didn't have that bear," Molly says.

The Rev shrugs. "Then I guess it's a good thing your boy here pissed off the whole city and you had to end up killing some dudes."

"Yeah. I guess so," Molly says.

"Shouldn't she be asleep right now, anyway?" I ask.

"I think tonight we can make an exception," Molly says. "Now bend over by the light so I can look at your neck."

I get down and Molly and the Rev both hover over me.

"Oh," Molly gasps.

"That is the fucking grossest thing I have ever seen, hands down," the Rev says.

Their disgust is well hidden.

"Describe it to me?" I ask. The itch is becoming overwhelming. "What does it look like?"

"I don't know, mate, kind of like you got shot, to be honest with ya. It's just this disgusting fucking hole, and it's all black goo inside. But . . . fuck me, it's like the goo is moving, I guess? Pulsating or some shit."

"What, like *it's alive?*" I cry out.

"Shit," the Rev says, and doesn't follow through with another response.

"Now, don't freak out, baby," Molly says.

Which obviously makes me freak the hell out.

"I said don't freak out!"

"I can't help it!" I shout. "This is pretty goddamn worthy of freaking out!"

Both Mol and the Rev hold me down on the floor, struggling to keep my body calm as they examine the animated cancer in my neck.

"Okay, fuck this," the Rev says. "Sorry, mate, but I can't help it. I'm gonna have to touch this thing."

"*What?* No, you don't *have* to touch it! Why the hell would you have to do something like that?"

"Dude, you aren't seeing what I'm seeing."

"Do not fucking touch it!"

"Okay, fine, I won't."

"Thank you." I sigh, attempting to breathe normally again.

The room goes silent save for our heavy breathing and Ezzy's curious giggling. Then the Rev's grip tightens around me.

"All right, so I lied."

"Whaa—AAARRRGGHHHFFFUUUUUCCCKKYOOO OUU."

It's like the back of my neck is a nuclear bomb and his finger is the detonator, and when they connect, total Armageddon erupts. His finger probes the source of my pain and every nerve in my body screams at once. He's found the single most agonizing spot in all of humanity, and he sure as hell isn't being gentle about it. All thought escapes me, my head filling with a fiery white blankness. Even my teeth shriek. I try to get up and run away, but it's no use. They're both on top of me now, and I'm just in too weak condition to fight. They're killing me. They're fucking murdering me just like I've murdered god knows how many other people. It is my time.

"Da-doo! Da-doo!" Ezzy shouts, crying now too, frightened at what is happening to her father. The side of my face pushed against the cold floor of the Rev's residence, I watch my daughter staring at me with absolute horror. She hugs her purple teddy tightly against her chest and I try to forge a smile to let her know everything is okay. Unfortunately, that smile is quickly replaced with another scream.

"GET OFF OF ME GODDAMMIT!"

"Hold on, you pussy." The Rev grunts from atop me. "Hold still, I almost got it . . . "

"Almost got *what?*"

"Just . . . hold still . . . almost . . . almost . . . I think I got it. Holy shit, I got it, I got it! Holy shit!"

A massive weight is pulled from my neck and my migraine evaporates like smoke through a vacuum. Molly and the Rev jump off me and I roll around on my back, panting like a dog. The Rev stands above me, holding something up to the light bulb, his face animated and intense. Molly's fallen on her ass, and is now scooting over to Ezzy, both of them crying.

"What is it? Tell me!" I try to stand, but I'm drowning in nausea. The room spins and I do what I can to hold on. *Hold on.*

The Rev looks at me, looks at the thing in his hand, then looks back at me. He appears as pale as I feel.

"Mate," he says softly, "this . . . uh, this . . . "

"What? What is it? What the fuck *is* it?"

"This is, uh, this is seriously, undoubtedly, the most fucked up thing I have ever seen. Besides your penis, of course."

"Shut up and just show me!"

He shrugs and turns his hands around, presenting something big and black dangling in his grip. It isn't just dangling, no, it's *squirming*. And then I realize he is holding the thing by one of its legs. One of its many, many legs.

He's holding a spider.

A spider which he has pulled out of my neck.

Out of *me*.

Oh my god.

My mind surrenders to darkness and the last thing I feel is the floor.

(interlude iv)

when the light returns, i find myself flat on my back. the rays of the sun glare down above me and penetrate through my body as if i am nothing more than a sad pathetic hologram. i know the sun is supposed to be hot and bright, yet it fazes my eyes no more than a small cobweb would my legs. i don't even want to get up, i'm content lying here on this sidewalk, never moving again. there are no concerns or worries or anything else bad when you're flat on your back looking up at the sky. there are no cult leaders tracking you down, no ghost doctors exploding, no funny bunny slippers, no hearts in coolers.

there aren't any spiders crawling out of your neck.

but of course, nothing good can last, nothing good can stay. soon my body begins to levitate, a mysterious set of god-like arms pushing me into a standing position, and once again i am on my feet, facing a world of oblivion. me #2 stands in front of me, leaning against the brick wall of some huge building, taking long drags off a cigarette. this downtown section is different than the area of downtown i've experienced. instead of a sea of vagabonds, the street is actually littered with passing automobiles. everyone drives past, not giving us the time of day. they have their own futures to live. we might as well be nothing more than floating orbs to them.

i turn back to me #2 and say, 'well, what are we doing here then?'

and of course he doesn't respond, because that would just make things easy.

the door to the building swings open and out strolls a man with his hair buzzed to the scalp. a demented grin extends across his scarred face as he jogs down steps. he carries a brown paper bag as he approaches my younger self against the wall.

please don't be another heart.

'you ready?' the man asks.

'you get it?' me #2 says.

'of course i fuckin' got it.' he holds up the brown paper bag for emphasis.

'well, then let me see. i need to know what one of these babies looks like.'

the man scans his surroundings, and reluctantly conceals the bag in his pants pocket. 'later. there's too many people around.'

me #2 sighs. 'pussy.'

'screw you, bobby.'

me #2 laughs and drops his cigarette butt to the ground. "let's go, dave. before . . . someone sees us."

i follow behind as the two men head down the sidewalk.

'how sure are you this thing is going to be here?' me #2 asks.

the other guy—dave—shrugs. 'lamb's never wrong about this shit.'

'yeah,' me #2 says, 'but wasn't lamb also the same guy who thought new england was a country?'

'yup,' dave says. 'also the same dude who butchered that one man's entire family after he spilled a cup of coffee in his lap. so, there's that.'

'fair enough.'

dave laughs and gives the past me a friendly, almost patronizing slap on the back. 'alls i'm sayin' is you gotta be careful what you say about certain people. don't matter if you don't think anyone can hear. stuff like that gets around, ya know? words travel with the wind, and in this city, it gets awfully windy.'

and just like that, the three of us are interrupted by a black sedan pulling up against the curb. me #2 tenses up, while dave doesn't seem to give it a second thought. however, once a man in a suit gets out of the car and slams the door behind him, dave decides that this new arrival may be of importance after all.

'yo, you gotta problem, buddy?' dave says. his smirk drops dead at the sight of the man's badge.

'detective marvin oasis,' the man in the suit says, approaching us with a bright, cheery grin. 'how's it hangin', boys?'

oasis.

now there's a name i recognize.

this is a dead man in front of us.

a man i've killed.

'what do you want?' me #2 says, giving the cop a mean stare. dave seems a little startled at past me's attitude with the officer. honestly, so am i.

oasis laughs. 'what do i want? you mean, like, right now? or in the long scheme of things? because, in the long scheme of things, well, i suppose i want indigo. but right now? boy, i tell ya, i could really go for a meatball sandwich.'

'we're not subway,' me #2 says. 'guess you better keep looking.'

oasis seems thoroughly amused. 'well, i was actually on my way to subway right now, when, by some magnificent stroke of luck, i happened to see you two trottin' down the sidewalk. and methinks, why, i know these two. they're always hanging out with jason lamb's lot. and if there's one person i truly can't stand, it's jason lamb. so, methinks, methinks . . . what are these two doing out here in the middle of the day, walking down my neighborhood for? i just wanted a meatball sub, but now i'm gonna have to actually do my job. which, honestly, is a damn shame. because, let me let you dirtbags in on a little secret: i fucking hate my job.'

he clocks his fist against dave's unsuspecting face, sending him to the ground shouting a rather inappropriate obscenity. me #2 leaps at the detective, but is blocked and thrown against a nearby trashcan. i just stand, watching in awe, thinking this dude is completely insane.

in a city of lunatics, who is the maddest?

'so, you all gonna start emptying those pockets, or am i gonna have to frisk ya?' the way he asks, it's like he would rather frisk us. like he enjoys doing things the hard way.

'i'm pretty sure this is against protocol, just a little bit,' me #2 says, standing back up.

'this is fucking bullshit, is what it is,' dave shouts, remaining seated on the ground, rubbing his jaw.

'are two criminals seriously giving me lip about breaking the law?' oasis laughs, nearly giggling. 'give me a break. now empty your pockets, and let's see what i can arrest you for.'

staring down the detective like he's the cause of all cancer in the world, me #2 digs into his pockets and pulls out a wallet, a lighter, and a pack of cigarettes.

so i do smoke, after all.

'unless tobacco has become illegal overnight, i doubt you'll find much cause there, bucko,' me #2 says. the cop takes one look at the stuff in his hands and smacks it to the ground.

then he looks down at dave. 'now you.'

the bleeding goon reluctantly empties his pockets: a wad of cash, matches, casino chips, a few gold chains, and a pack of gum. he shrugs. 'that's it. i swear.'

'bullshit,' oasis says. 'you don't have that big ol' jacket on for no reason. cough up the goods, baby.'

dave gives me #2 a look, as if asking what to do, and he just shrugs, implying to go ahead. and i'm standing here in the middle of all this just praying to god he isn't about to pull out a harvested heart.

just walk away, oasis. before it's too late.

'fine,' dave says, reaching in his jacket and coming back out with the brown paper bag. oasis snags it from the goon's hand.

'here we go,' he says, opening it greedily. he peeks inside, then dumps the bag's contents out into his other hand. a small, silver whistle drops into his palm.

he looks at the whistle calmly, examining its every inch. i'm right in front of him, looking at it just as perplexed. what the hell?

oasis drops the whistle to the ground. i'm pretty sure i'm the only one who notices the deep gust of breath dave chokes back as he watches it bounce off the sidewalk.

'a whistle,' oasis mumbles, no longer amused.

'uh, yeah, ya know,' dave says. 'in case someone tries to rape me. i keep it on me at all times.'

oasis dismisses the goon and glares at me #2, who has now taken the role of the one smiling. 'are you fucking kidding me?' the cop says.

'never,' me #2 says. 'now, if you don't mind . . . '

'screw it,' oasis says, and gets back in the sedan. he flips us the middle finger as he pulls away.

me #2 picks up the whistle and holds it closely. 'a goddamn whistle. this is what you were so scared about people seeing?'

'hey, man, that is one powerful whistle,' dave says, grunting as he climbs back up to his feet. he takes the whistle and stuffs it in his pocket, while me #2 re-collects the items oasis had knocked to the ground.

'what a dick,' dave says. 'no wonder cops get such a bad rap.'

'well, to be fair, we are pretty dangerous criminals,' me #2 says.

'true.'

'i mean, just look at that fucking whistle. hardcore, man.'

'oh, go eat a bag of dicks,' dave says, walking again. 'let's get moving.'

and that's what they do, and i of course follow. but all i'm thinking about is how oasis looked back at the river, with a bunch of bullet holes in him. he didn't seem so tough then.

what the hell happened?

the faster we walk, the more i notice how the passing cars fade from reality. it's like the people back at that bar, how they weren't really there, at least not to me. the cars have done the same thing—they've transformed into these floating orbs.

who are these people? where are they going?

where are we going?

i keep asking this, yet nobody is answering. no one hears me. i am alone.

'are we alone?' dave asks, stopping suddenly.

me #2 looks behind us and nods. 'uh, yeah. as alone as we're gonna get.'

'just get the feeling we're not.'

'just me,' me #2 says, and i can't help but laugh.

'there's something i still don't get,' me #2 says. "why are we even needed, in all of this, when there's harvies to do the dirty work? i mean, they do the harvesting, so why do we transport the shit? why can't they just do that, too?"

dave shrugs. 'they aren't exactly the best behaved around humans.'

'meaning?'

'what do you think?' he says. 'anyway, it doesn't matter. we're here.'

me #2 and i look up at the same time toward an abandoned warehouse towering above us. most of the windows are broken, and those that aren't have been colored black by dust and neglect.

133

'of course this is it,' me #2 says. 'it's only the creepiest damn building in the whole city. what other place could it be?'

'lamb was very specific, this is where . . . it'll be.'

me #2 sighs. "hey, at least we have a whistle."

there's obviously no one else here right now. maybe come nightfall, things will change. it looks like an ideal home to vagrants. and what's wrong with that? everybody needs a place to sleep. it doesn't seem like the building has any other use, after all.

'isn't this going to be dangerous?' past me asks. 'something as evil as this thing, i'd think we would be more prepared than just a whistle. like a gun, or something.'

dave shakes his head. 'nah, a bullet would just whiz right past one of these things. this whistle is what can control it. uh, so i'm told.'

'hmm,' me #2 says. 'and how, again, did lamb know that it'd be here, in this building of all places?'

'lamb didn't know—indigo did. and indigo told lamb.'

'ah.' me #2 nods. 'but, uh, how reliable is this indigo fella? i mean, none of us have even seen him.'

'i have.'

we've reached the end of the first floor, and now begin the short trek up the steps. they grunt with each motion, yet to me, this doesn't feel like exercise at all. it's like i'm slowly gliding behind, a rope tied around my waist, with my doppelganger pulling me along.

'bullshit,' me #2 says.

'it's true,' dave says.

'bull . . . shit.'

'no, really.'

'when?'

'a few months back. i was in the casino, watching the fight. i noticed that one room behind the cage, up on that balcony? the curtain there was waving, like someone had just been up there. then i think i saw a hand. pretty sure i saw a hand.'

134

'and that's your amazing indigo sighting story?' me #2 asks.

'better than your amazing indigo sighting story.'

'well, i don't give a crap who lamb and indigo think they are: whoever gave them their intel is a goddamn fool. this place is empty.'

and of course, like the gun at a racetrack, this marks the start of the race.

a huge gust of wind suddenly runs rampant through the room. i know this not from the sensation, but from all the dirt and trash blowing around like a greasy tornado. the hairs on me #2's head swirl around comically, lashing him across the face.

'what the hell—?'

a loud shriek infiltrates the room, and in comes a huge blur—something i actually mistake as a literal tornado, before i realize that it's just another man running through the room. a man dressed all in white.

'oh my god, do you think that's him?' dave yells over the screeching.

'of course that's fucking him,' me #2 yells back, and watches as the white tornado man throws dave clear across the room, knocking him on his ass.

'get him,' dave says, throwing the whistle toward us. me #2 attempts to catch it, fumbles, then hugs it to his chest—all the while staring wide-eyed at this strange creature. staring like we just saw something we didn't actually believe existed. staring like our whole world has been flipped upside down.

i try to hide behind a table, then realize the irrationality of my fear. i'm just here for the show, after all. this isn't my action scene. not anymore, at least.

the white blur of a man knocks a few more things to the ground and zips down the steps. me #2 gives dave a confused, hopeless look, and says, 'well, shit, now what?'

'go get him!' dave screams. 'if he gets away, lamb will

castrate us both! my damn ankle is sprained, so it's up to you.'

'why do i get the impression that your ankle is actually fine?'

'now is not the time for questions, bobby.'

me #2 shakes his head. 'typical.'

he runs down the steps.

well, i'm not following him. there's no way in hell.

but i'm not given a choice. standing here, ghost-arms crossed over my chest, i am smacked in the face with the huge, mighty dick of gravity, and fall straight to the floor. being the helpless victim that i am, i can do nothing but scream and shout for the assistance of people who can't hear me as my body melts into the hardwood floor and leaks out below, dripping down to the first story. the room spins for a moment, and then i regain sense of vision.

i am not meant to stay away.

i am meant to see.

standing in the main lobby, i find myself face-to-face with another one of those doctors. the ones that . . . like to smell. and this one is smelling me. despite not really existing here, the goddamn thing is smelling me. this . . . harvester. this harvey. it knows i'm here.

it recognizes my odor.

and the worst part is, i can feel the air trickling against my skin from its nostrils.

i can feel it smelling me, oh my god, i can feel it.

'get away,' i whisper. 'please just get away.'

and the thing, this doctor, it says something to me. not to past me, but to ME me.

it says, 'kill him.'

and that's when me #2 stumbles down the steps, whistle in mouth. he blows down hard, and even though i don't hear the tune it makes, i can tell by the harvey's facial expression that it hears plenty. its mouth extends wide in a merciless scream, eyeballs pulsating like a black sun.

and then it explodes.
just like before.
me #2 watches the same way i watched the other harvey self-destruct at the drugstore: horrified.
i look down at where the harvey had just been standing, and i see no signs of its existence. in fact, there is nothing on the ground at all.
nothing . . . except for a carpet of black spiders.

chapter fifteen

Everything fades. Return to present and it's one of the same spiders that's just been pulled from out of my neck. The one that's now on the ground, running amok in the Rev's dubious excuse of a residence. I puke a little in my mouth as we watch it scattering along the hard concrete floor.

Meanwhile, the Rev has jumped on top of his futon, shielding himself with a stained pillow. His accent vanishes as he shouts, "Kill that fucking thing!"

Molly backs up against the wall, wide-eyed and trembling.

I crawl toward the fleeing neck-demon, grabbing at it with sweaty hands, but it's too fast. It dodges my every attempt, like it's able to predict each move before I even make it.

"What are you doing?" Molly says. "Get away from that thing—Ezzy, no!"

I see it happening, but there's nothing I can do to stop it.

The spider redirects its course straight for Ezzy, freezing time in its place. All I'm thinking is, I can't let that thing bite her. Who knows what kind of crazy poisons it's carrying. Who knows what this thing even is. It's more than a spider. It's more than any of us can ever possibly know.

Please, no . . .

But before the spider can sink its fangs into my daughter, Ezzy swoops her hand down, picks the creature up, and bites its head clean off.

She tosses the decapitated body behind her, like a banana peel.

We all stare at her, blankly watching as she chews on the spider head. She nods in approval.

"Yum, Da-doo, that's yum!" she exclaims, and more vomit introduces itself to the inside of my mouth.

"I think I'm going to be sick," Molly says.

I swallow, grimacing. "Way ahead of you."

The Rev jumps off the couch, excited. He picks up Ezzy and swings her in a circle, the two of them laughing and smiling. "*Yes!*" he shouts. "Now *that* is how you fucking kill a spider!"

"Language!" Molly says, taking our daughter from the madman with a mohawk. "I can't believe she did that. Good Lord."

"I know," I whisper.

"Do you think she got anything from it? Like some of its poison?"

"I don't know, Mol. I don't know."

She cradles Ezzy close to her chest, rocking her to sleep, and I'm sitting on the floor and all I'm able to think about is how that harvey had exploded.

How all that was left were a bunch of spiders.

I look back at Ezzy, who is a second away from drifting off.

What just happened?

"All right, do you guys think this is a good point to wonder what the hell a spider was doin' in your neck, or what? Because I can't think of a better time," the Rev says.

We're all sitting on the floor now, Ezzy on the futon, sound asleep. I wish we were all passed out, too. My body can only go so much longer before it randomly combusts like the harvey had exploded back at the drugstore, back at the warehouse. But there's still too much to talk about.

Specifically, the whole "spider in my goddamn neck" dilemma.

"Obviously it's been in there all night," I say, and it suddenly occurs to me that I have no idea how much time has passed since awakening at the river. This has been the longest night in the history of all nights. Outside, the sun is only just now rising. Our sleep schedules are going to be so screwed up, it's not even funny. "It's been in my neck all this time . . . just waiting for you to pull it out."

"But why?" Molly asks.

"Maybe it didn't want to be pulled out, ya know?" the Rev says. "Like, I dunno, maybe it wanted to stay in your neck."

"Why the hell would it want to do that?" I say, rubbing the hole in the back of my neck and wincing at the pain.

"No clue. Maybe it's comfortable, I don't know, I've never hung out in some dude's neck before."

"Either way, it's dead now," Molly says, looking at our sleeping infant.

"That thing was something else," I say. "I get the feeling it was the cause of my shot memory. Someone *put* that inside me. I just know it."

"Lamb?"

"Who else?"

"Maybe Indigo, dude," the Rev says.

"You know," I say, "I keep hearing that name, but nobody's telling me who the fuck he is."

"All right," the Rev says, "since you're still all brain stupid, I'll let this one slide. Ya know how Lamb seems like this big tough cunt, ya? That is, until you blew his face off. Well he was an ant compared to Indigo. Indigo practically fuckin' runs this city. The police listen to him. He calls the shots. You know that casino at the edge of the city, on Collie Hill?"

I just look at him stupidly. "No, I have no idea what you're talking about."

"Jesus, dude, at least pretend," the Rev says. "Look,

there's this huge fuckin' casino, all right? It's on top of a huge fuckin' hill. I guess you could call it Indigo's lair, if you were a nerdy virgin. Normal men call it a fuckin' casino, and it just so happens to be the place Indigo never leaves. Seriously, I don't know if he's on house arrest or what, man."

"So he's rich."

"Straight fuckin' balla."

"You think he's behind this shit?" I ask.

"If there's shit going on, Indigo can pretty much be guaranteed to be behind it," the Rev says. "He makes it his business to be behind it. That's common knowledge, mate. Get your bearings together."

I crack my neck and instantly regret it, the pain from the spider hole inflamed again. "So Indigo wants me dead. The man who controls the city, and everyone in it."

"Most of everyone," the Rev says. "And yeah."

"Then what are our options?"

The Rev shrugs. "We gotta get the fuck out of this city. Out of this state. Shit, we need to be in a whole new country. Even that may not be far enough. Who knows how far Indigo's reach goes."

"All right, fine, we'll leave. You have any idea how the hell we do that with his goons everywhere?"

The Rev thinks for a moment. Molly cradles our child in her arms. I wonder if the spider's head has already digested. What did it taste like? Will this provoke a new food fetish for my daughter? I don't want to know the answers to any of these questions.

"Hey!" the Rev says. "You know Jed, right? Oh, wait, of course you don't. Anyway we know a guy named Jed who'd be perfect for our . . . uh, predicament. His special skill is, er, making people go away. You know, disappear."

"What the hell do you mean by that?"

The Rev gives me an annoyed look, as if I'm intentionally playing dumb. "I mean he gets rid of dead bodies."

"But we're not dead."

"So?" the Rev says. "Can't be that different. If anyone will know how to sneak us out of this shit hole, it'll be Jed. Trust me on this."

"Okay." I nod and walk over to Molly and our daughter, wrapping my arms around them. Lips connect to her neck as I whisper, "What do you think? You up for this?"

"The alternative would be death," Molly says. "Of course I'm up for it. What other choice do we have?"

"I'm sorry I've done this to you and Ezzy. I honestly can say I don't know what I was thinking, but I was a dumbass."

She smiles, kisses me softly on the cheek. "But you're trying to fix it now, and that's all that matters."

Yawning, I return the smile. "We all need to get some sleep first. I'm about to pass out."

"Good idea, mate," the Rev says. He jumps on the futon and promptly falls asleep, within seconds.

"Did he really just do that?" I ask, still standing in the same spot.

Molly shrugs. "You're adorable when you don't have a memory."

My eyes open, and I find myself sitting on the cold floor of the Rev's "house", leaning against the wall. Molly lays in my lap, and Ezzy lays in hers. Thanks to the lack of sun inside this storage unit, there's no telling how long we've been asleep.

The Rev sits on the futon reading a book called *The Anarchist's Cookbook*. It sounds familiar. I don't think it's actually about food.

"Hey, Rev," I say.

'Yeah, mate?"

"What's your real name?"

He laughs. "I've known you for how many years now?

What makes you think I'm gonna tell you now? I am the Rev and that's all I'll ever be."

"That's kind of sad."

"Eh," he says, "it is what it is."

"Exactly how long have we known each other?"

The Rev shrugs. "I've been way too high and drunk to keep track of that, mate."

My soul craves answers. It is never satisfied. "Was I a good friend?"

The Rev laughs at me, looking up from his book this time. "Absolutely not, but neither was I. And there's nothing wrong with that at all."

"I guess," I say, disappointed.

"So are we gonna get the fuck out of here or what?" the Rev says.

Once Molly and Ezzy wake up a few minutes later, we gather our belongings, take care of our bathroom needs (he has . . . buckets), and slip out of the storage unit. The sun lingers westward.

"This Jed, how far away does he live?" I ask, readjusting my grip with Ezzy, hugging her arms tight so she doesn't fall off my shoulders. She's having a hell of a time. We really suck at being incognito.

"He likes to remain secluded. We'll have to take the mono."

Molly taps me on the back and says, "Uh, what are we going to do if one of the, uh, you know, *bad guys,* catches us walking out like this. I mean, we're not exactly hiding. We're kind of right out in the open."

"There's not exactly many other options, now is there, Mol?" the Rev says. "The man lives this way. So, we have to go this way. I mean, for Christ's sake, what do you expect us to do, fly there?"

Molly shrugs, acting like the victim of an unannounced crime. "No, that isn't what I mean, it just seems that there has to be a better way to go about this. Like, we should at least be wearing disguises or something."

"You know," I say, "she does have a point."

The Rev sighs. "No one is gonna fuckin' recognize us."

"Hey, Rev!" a random guy on the street shouts. "How ya doin', you ugly sumbitch?"

"Okay," the Rev says. "No one except for him."

"Rev!" he shouts again, nearing. He wears only a bathrobe. The smile across his face makes me doubt he's much of a threat, but I stay on my guard nonetheless. "Where ya been, dude? Brown and me climbed the taco stand and dropped acid. It was beautiful."

"I was fightin' neck spiders and throwing babies into dumpsters, Carl," the Rev says.

Carl nods. "Ah, well, that's cool too. But hey, check it out. These lame as fuck dudes were around here earlier, askin' about you. They seemed real fuckin' pissed."

We all stop walking. Carl gasps at the amount of attention suddenly directed toward him. "Whoa, you guys, your eyeballs are strange."

"What dudes?" the Rev asks. "They were asking about *me?*"

Carl nods. "I don't know, man. Like, dudes from the casino, ya know? All business and stiff, walkin' like they got sticks of dynamite up their assholes."

"Hey!" Molly says. "There's a baby present."

Carl notices Ezzy and gasps again. "Oh my god, I thought that was a ball of cotton candy."

"Well, it's not. It's a baby," Molly says.

"Assholes," Ezzy says.

"Aww," Carl says. "That's adorable!"

"Ezzy!" Molly shouts.

Ezzy laughs.

"Wait," the Rev says, holding his hand up. "What did they ask?"

Carl shrugs. "Just like, if I knew where you live, and if I saw anybody with you lately. Like a dude with rabbit slippers on, or a redhead with a . . . baby." He looks at my feet and nods. "Yeah, like those."

"They're funny bunnies," I tell him.

"They're terrifying. Why are they looking at me like that? Why do they hate me?"

"Shut up about the goddamn slippers," Molly says. "What did you tell these people?"

"Well, I'm not about to rat out my boy Rev," Carl says. "So I told them y'all were shooting up down on Hemrock."

The Rev smiles. "Good thinkin', my man."

"How far away is Hemrock?" I ask.

"I don't know, about twenty minutes from here," the Rev says.

"And how long ago did you talk to these people, Carl?"

"I no longer have any concept of numbers," Carl says. "All I know are colors."

"Uh, all right."

"They were here, maybe, I dunno, eighty oranges, two and a half turquoises ago."

"Oh shit," the Rev says. "They'll be back soon then, even more pissed off."

"We gotta move," I say. "Let's go."

We leave Carl and begin walking again. Carl shouts after us, "Hey, wait! I still have some acid left. We could all drop it together and have an orgy. Come on, guys!"

"I'm okay with that if you are," the Rev says, slowing down.

"Just keep moving," I tell him, pushing him along.

The Rev scoffs. "Like we've never been in an orgy together before."

Molly stops. "What the fuck?"

"Orgy!" Ezzy shouts, gleefully clapping her hands together and giggling.

chapter sixteen

The sun boils my eyeballs and I yearn for darkness to return. Ezzy sits on my shoulders as we walk through the traffic of vagrants shuffling down the street. With the moon absent and the sun taking its place, these people look even gloomier. Drool drips from their dropped jaws and their pupils swirl in a misty white. They're all high as fuck and maybe there's nothing wrong with that.

We pass an overturned car. Inside there's a family of corpses. I stop and look at the driver's decomposed arm hanging from the window. The majority of the flesh has been torn from the bone. How long have they been here? How many mouths did these corpses feed?

"Ezzy doesn't need to see this," Molly says, and pushes me along.

A man two blocks down holds a sign with one hand that reads "CONUNDRAE WILL RISE" and he stares at us, smiling while he jacks off with his other hand. I return the stare and try my hardest to initiate my telekinesis. I visualize him flinging from the sidewalk and smashing into the abandoned building behind him. But nothing happens. He continues standing there, pleasuring himself, until the Rev punches him in the face and he collapses.

I don't understand these mind powers. I don't understand anything. The more I think about it, the greater my headache. Even with the spider out of me, my brain throbs something fierce. What the *fuck* was the spider doing inside me, anyway? The same kind of spider I saw in those harvies, too. Shit, this isn't good. None of this is good. What if there are other spiders inside me that they didn't get out?

Molly and the Rev don't know any more than I do. Those who can answer my questions want me dead. If I want to know anything, I'll have to confront my own killers. I can't do this. I can't fucking do this. I can risk my life to understand my past, or I can flee to save my future.

Which do I care about more?

Ezzy runs her tiny fingers through my hair, giggling. "Faster, Da-doo, faster!"

Her. Ezzy. Molly. They're who I care about.

The past is only as important as I make it. Just let go. Forget about it. I already have. Just forget I've forgotten and move on.

We arrive at the monorail station about half a mile later. The tracks are empty but people surround the area on both sides, awaiting the mono's arrival. We find an empty spot next to the railing. I attempt to lean against the handrail but immediately draw back once I feel how loosely screwed in it is to the concrete. It'd only take the weight of someone as small as Ezzy to knock the entire structure down to the street below.

"Why are we like this?" I ask, gesturing at the crowd of motionless zombies around us. "What the hell is wrong with everybody?"

The Rev stares at me a moment, figuring my brain out. "This is just the way shit is, man. You're acting like you're a goddamn time travellin' asshole instead of some dude who lost his noggin'."

"None of this feels right, is all. We're all so sad and miserable looking. There's no structure to this city. It's all ugly."

Molly caresses my cheek. "We aren't all ugly."

"You're right, though," the Rev says. "Shit wasn't always so bad. But drugs, man, they fuck you up. Indigo is a powerful motherfucker. Sometimes, power is all that matters. That fuckin' cult, dude. It got out of hand. When we were kids, shit, it was only just starting. Look at it now."

"Why can't anybody stop him?" I ask. "All these junkies and dealers, they easily outnumber him."

The Rev shrugs. "Maybe they don't mind it. Hell, I'm okay with it most of the time. Beats havin' coppers getting in your shit twenty-four-seven, ya know? We're pretty much free. As long as we don't piss off the big man, which you seem to have done."

"I wonder what I did."

"Probably fucked his girl or something."

Molly turns and slaps my chest. "You better not have!"

I wince, rubbing my chest. "Jesus Christ, you know I didn't."

"Do *you* know you didn't?"

She has a good point.

Up ahead, the mono nears. The vagabonds rise as it slows to a stop at our station. Once the doors slide open, a wave of fresh, dirty faces pour from out of the box and drift down the station's steps, merging with the crowds in the streets. We push our way through the people and manage to find some empty seats close together.

Ezzy sits on my knee, eyes widening in awe at all the interesting characters passing us. I rub her back and take comfort in how much warmth such a little creature can provide. When I woke at the river, I was on the verge of death. I was a cloud of chaos, an ocean of oblivion. I was extinction.

But now that I've found my family, the thought of death couldn't be less welcoming. Every second further I'm alive is another second I get to spend with them, and I don't intend on running out of seconds anytime soon.

So fuck Indigo. Fuck Lamb and his blown-off face. Fuck this whole goddamn city. I have Molly. I have Ezzy. Hell, I even have the Rev. I don't need anybody or anything else. Not all questions are meant to be answered.

The monorail takes off and we're in motion. It moves

slowly, like it's uncertain of its own stability. We coast through the city and I hold Ezzy up against the window so she can see the passing buildings. She points and gasps, saying, "Ooh, Da-doo, look, look!"

And I tell her, "I'm looking, baby girl. I'm looking."

As we gain distance from the station, the buildings look less and less depressing. The boarded-up windows cease to exist and a few of the buildings even appear to be fully functional businesses. Cars replace the vagabonds on the streets, although the majority of them look like they're about to break down any moment. A part of me is relieved that the entire city isn't full of drug addicts overdosing in the middle of the street, but another part of me knows the same shit is still happening—it's just better hidden here.

The mono picks up speed and the buildings zip past faster. Ezzy waves against the window, saying, "Bye-bye, bye-bye."

Soon we'll be saying bye-bye to the whole city.

"We get off at the next stop," the Rev says.

I nod. "How much of a walk once we leave the station?"

"Maybe twenty, thirty minutes. Not too far."

"And he'll be able to help us?"

"If he can't, then I don't know who would. Jed makes people disappear. It's what he does. He's the bloke we need, trust me."

"I don't really understand that, though," I say, looking at the people around us. "Why would anyone need his services? Seems like somebody could walk up and kill everybody at this station, and nobody would give a shit."

"Yeah, true, but there's some people you simply *don't* kill, though, and if you do, you do whatever it fuckin' takes to make sure nobody finds out."

"Like who?"

"Like people who work for Indigo."

A few minutes later the monorail slows to a stop and we get off. The station is nearly identical to the last one. The doors outside are surrounded by barely functioning sacks of flesh waiting to board once we leave. They push past us and glue themselves to empty seats. We stand at the station a moment, stretching our legs and preparing for the walk ahead of us.

A man wearing a diaper crafted out of soggy newspapers approaches us. He stops in front of Molly and grins, revealing black teeth. "Hey there, baby," he says.

"Fuck off," I tell him.

He shoots his head up and looks at me, still grinning. "Anybody lookin' for some action?" He grabs his badly concealed crotch and gives it a tug for emphasis.

I move toward him and he leaps back, holding his hands up and laughing. "Hey there, hey there, I was just kiddin'. I's sorry."

I don't say anything, just keep walking toward him, a look in my eyes that tells him I won't hesitate to rip his head off. He gets the hint and runs away from us, screaming that we're all a bunch of humorless assholes.

As he runs, I stare at him and try to fling him over the railing of the station using my mind powers. Nothing happens.

Molly sighs. "I hate this city."

I turn back around toward her. "We won't be here much longer. I promise."

"I'll hold you to that," she says.

I bend down and pick up Ezzy, then look at the Rev. "Well, where to?"

The Rev points at the darkening sky and shouts, "To the moon, Alice!"

Molly sighs again.

The forest we walk through to get to Jed's hideout reminds me of the forest I ran through when I first woke up at the river. The mosquitos are bastards and every fourth step is a puddle of soggy soil. I remember how I'd ran through the forest, in pure darkness, not knowing what I was, where I was going, or even what my name had been. Now here I am again in a similar forest, only this time I have my family by my side, and the world is a little less miserable.

"Ouch, Da-doo, ouch!" Ezzy shouts from atop my shoulders, and I realize a tree branch just smacked her in the face.

"Jesus Chris, Bobby," Molly says. "You almost decapitated our child."

"Almost," I tell her, "*almost*."

"Shut up," the Rev says. "We're here."

"Where?" I ask. All I see are trees and more trees. "There's nothing here."

"Dude," the Rev says. "There's a big ass cabin right in front of us."

"What? No there isn't." Then I take a step to the left, and now that a huge tree isn't obstructing my vision, a cabin comes into view. "Oh. Never mind."

"Okay, now we have to be very careful," the Rev says. "There's like a fifty-fifty chance this guy will shoot us for trespassing."

Molly stops walking. "*What?*"

The Rev shrugs. "It just depends on how drunk he is."

"Why didn't we call ahead or something?" I ask.

"Dude doesn't have a phone anymore. He shot it. For trespassing."

chapter seventeen

"Sure, I've once eaten a human, and yeah, it didn't taste too bad, if I don't say so myself." Jed finishes off his beer and asks if we want another. We all just sit in his kitchen, staring at him, wondering why he chose to randomly bring up cannibalism.

"Listen," he says, "I'm not sayin' eatin' humans ain't wrong, but when it's you and some other guy and there ain't no other food, it's either eat or be eaten, and me, I'm gonna eat."

Jed rubs his rather large stomach, smiling.

The Rev nods. "Sure, sure."

Molly gives me a look telling me she desperately wants to flee this lunatic's cabin, and I respond with a similar stare.

"So," I say, clearing my throat, "do you think you can help us?"

Jed leans forward, a new beer in hand. "You really don't remember ever meeting me before?"

I shake my head. "I don't remember a whole lot of anything, to be honest. I don't know what was done to me, but it seriously screwed me up."

"I can take a guess."

"I knew it," the Rev says. "He's swallowed so much sperm that his brain finally exploded."

I elbow the Rev in the ribs and nod at Jed. "What do you think happened?"

The cabin is smaller than I expected, but comfortable.

The floors are covered in bearskin rugs and the walls are decorated with the decapitated heads of deer. The heads stare at us, frozen mid-scream. The majority of the living room floor is littered with old, disintegrating paperbacks. Most of the book covers feature barely dressed women and men wearing big trench coats, much like the one I stole at the river. When we arrived and told him why we were here, he led us through the living room, down the short hallway, and into the kitchen. He explained that it was the only room in the house with enough seating for all of us, plus it was the closest spot to the beer. The kitchen is small and forgettable. A sink. A refrigerator. A cabinet and pantry. A dining table. I stare at it all and instantly fade it out.

Jed sips his beer. "Well, I mean, come on, just think about it for a moment. You wake up in the middle of nowhere, naked, head throbbing, no memory, a bunch of dead folks around you. You find out you did something wrong, you 'screwed over the wrong people', as that dickhead Lamb said. Can't you piece it together?"

The room falls silent. Everybody waits for me to respond, but I don't know. I don't know anything. Maybe it's obvious to Jed, but I haven't a fucking clue.

"Well?" the Rev says. "Is someone gonna say something or what? You're all freaking me out."

Jed sits back in his seat, relaxed. He stares at me, awaiting a response I'm not going to give. After a few more moments of waiting, he says, "All right, let's talk about the harvesters. The harvies."

"Okay, well, what about them?" I ask.

"Well, as you done already described them," Jed says, "they're almost like ghosts. White, pale, generally pretty fuckin' spooky lookin'. But why do they exist?"

"Oh!" Molly says, sitting forward. "They *harvest!* It's right there in the name."

"Well, yeah," Jed says. "But *what* do they harvest?"

I think about the cooler back at the drugstore. "Organs. They harvest human organs."

Jed nods, smiling. "Right you are, Bobby. How do they harvest, though? What makes them so special? Why can't just any guy do the job? Why does Indigo need these things specifically?"

I stare at him, waiting for him to answer.

"Because," he says, "harvies possess a rather special gift. A regular human, they cut a person's heart out, it goes bad within a matter of hours—if that. But a harvey, well, harvies are different. They're able to pull a heart out of a human body and still allow it to continue beating. With a harvey, life continues, even if the organ in question is no longer connected to where it's supposed to be connected."

"How?" Molly asks.

And suddenly everything makes sense. Jed doesn't have to explain any further. I know what he's going to say before he even says it. I stand up, pacing the living room of the cabin.

"Because," I finally say, "harvies are telekinetic."

Jed's smile widens. "Indeed so. They are able to force organs to live whether they want to or not. They possess powers unlike anything we've ever seen before. They look at a heart and tell it to beat and it beats. They are gods. They are monsters. They are insane."

I sit back down, silent. My thoughts run wild.

"Which," Jed says, "as you've probably already considered, is quite similar to your little mind problem. Seeing as, like the harvies, you're also telekinetic."

"Oh, shit," Molly says.

"Oh, shit is right," I whisper.

"What?" the Rev says. "I don't get it."

"I'm a harvey," I say. "Or, at least, *some kind* of harvey. I don't know. *I don't fucking know.*"

"My guess is," Jed says, "is Indigo tried turnin' you into one of his little pets, and something went wrong, so they dumped you in the river. But you weren't completely dead like they thought. And now, despite your memory loss, you still have some of the abilities of a harvey. Like the telekinesis."

"What about the spider?" I ask. "What does that have to do with me? Why was it *inside of me?*"

Jed shrugs. "I have no fucking idea, man. Maybe spiders have something do with harvies. I don't know."

"I have this memory," I say. "Me and this other guy, we were hunting one of these harvies. I don't know why, but we were. We had this whistle. For some reason, the whistle really fucked them up, like it deconstructed it or something. A whistle, of all things. I don't know. Like any of this makes sense, right?"

"Right," the Rev says. "Clearly you're insane."

"That's okay, though," I say. "I'd have to be insane to believe any of this shit. But anyway, once we found this . . . this harvey, and we used the whistle, the thing, the fucking *thing* blew up, and in its place were these spiders. The same kind of spider that you guys pulled from my neck."

Jed nods, as if everything I'm saying makes sense, which means he's probably psychotic.

"So," he says, "the connection's there, we just don't understand *why* the spiders affect both you and the harvies. I ain't no scientist, so maybe this would all seem obvious to someone smarter than me. Hell, maybe you'll get a chance to ask Indigo yourself." He pauses a moment, then smiles. "But not if I can help it."

"To be honest," the Rev says, finishing off his beer, "I don't even believe this fucker *does* have any powers. I haven't seen shit. Dude's screwing with all of us."

I kick his leg with the bottom of my funny bunny slipper. "I told you already, I can't control it. It only seems to happen as a last resort, like some sort of self-defense mechanism. You dick."

The Rev rubs his leg and looks at Molly. "What about you, then? Have you seen Bobby 'in action'?"

Molly giggles. "Well."

"I mean the mind voodoo." He shakes his head. "For fuck's sake."

She pauses, thinking about it, then says, "Actually, no . . . "

"Bullshit," I say. "Back at the apartment, I broke the window, then I crushed that asshole's windpipe."

"I didn't really see it, though."

"Mol, you were right there. How couldn't you have seen it?"

Molly shrugs. "I'm not saying you didn't, I'm just saying I didn't see it."

"Well, that settles it," the Rev says. "Bobby's making it all up."

"Oh, shut up." I kick him again, then stand up. "I'm not making this shit up. I don't know why I would."

The Rev laughs. "I'm just messing around, mate. Calm down."

I ignore him and look down at Jed. "Well, what are you thinking then? What's the plan?"

"Well, the only way y'all are gonna get out of here alive is by the tunnels. Just too risky travellin' the streets. Indigo has eyes everywhere."

"And that's safe?" I ask. "The tunnels, I mean. We can leave the city that way?"

"Of course," Jed says. "That's how the Refragatio gets around without getting caught."

I stop breathing for a moment, then clear my throat. "The Refragatio?"

Jed doesn't need to explain who they are. I step away from everybody, ignoring their comments. I know the Refragatio. I hadn't remembered them until Jed brought them up, but now? Yeah. I know the Refragatio about as good as I know oxygen.

Fuck. How could I have ever forgotten?

(interlude v)

in a cage, trapped like a rat. i've been caught. the bastards finally got me.

the cage is not small by any stretch. it could easily hold a dozen people. it resides in the center of an expansive room occupied by at least three hundred patrons. they sit and stand around the cage, drinking liquor and watching me. only they're not watching me, they're watching the two other men standing in the cage. the two shirtless, shoeless men beating the shit out of each other.

the crowd cheers for the two men to tear each other to pieces. they stand on either side of me, driving their fists through my ghost body and into each other's faces. for a moment i'm convinced one of the men fighting is me #2, but after a second glance, neither one seems all too familiar.

i step out of their way so they can continue the fight, even though they seem perfectly content brawling with me between them. one of the men locks the other in a headlock and drops him to the floor. the crowd yells, wild with excitement.

blood is their entertainment. violence is their orgasm. death is their paradise.

i see me #2 sitting outside the cage at a table by himself, drinking a beer. he watches the fight without really watching. his eyes stare at the cage but his mind is elsewhere, lost someplace dark and disturbing.

i move away from the brawling duo and press myself against the cage bars. i barely have to use any force to squeeze through metal and plop out the other side. me #2 shows no sign of disturbance as i land directly on his table and fall through it, my head landing softly on his crotch. when i eventually crawl out from under the table and stand up, me #2 has finished his drink and is just sitting there, looking at the empty glass. the crowd cheers as more blood is shed in the cage and me #2 doesn't flinch.

what are you thinking?

where in time are we now?

i look around the room and i realize this is a casino, only not any casino, but THE casino. the casino where hell parties and heaven disintegrates.

indigo's casino.

what the fuck are we doing here?

i try to leave, but of course i can't. now that i'm by me #2, i'm stuck here, like a fly in a spider's web. my legs are useless until he makes the first move. but he doesn't look like he's planning on moving any time soon. he's too preoccupied with the empty glass, almost like he's trying to conjure more booze with his mind. and, fuck, maybe he can. if i can move objects and make heads explode, then maybe i can create liquor, too.

you drunk bastard. you pathetic lush. do something. your whole life is about to fall apart. get the fuck out of here, man. find molly and ezzy and hug them and pack your shit and get the hell out of this miserable city before it eats you alive.

but he isn't listening. i'm not really here. maybe i'm not even at jed's cabin. maybe i'm dead and i'm just living a mirage. soon reality's gonna vaporize and there will be nothing but beautiful darkness.

but darkness isn't so beautiful when i can be holding my daughter instead. so, darkness can go fuck itself.

a man in a blue uniform approaches us. he clears his

throat and taps me #2 on the shoulder. me #2 spins around, drunk and startled.

'what?' me #2 says, making a fist.

the man laughs at me #2's limp fists and says, 'lamb's called for you. he needs your help.'

'fuck lamb.'

'i'd rather not,' the man says. 'anyway, him and the rest of 'em are down in the boiler room.'

'what the hell are they doing there?'

'having a circle jerk,' he says. 'how the hell would i know? he radioed me and said to bring your ass down there—so, get your ass down there.'

'bite me.'

'another time.'

the man walks away, leaving us alone at the table. me #2 sits there a moment, staring at the empty glass a little longer, then sighs.

'shit.'

he rises and stumbles through the crowd of gamblers. his magnetic hook latches onto my chest and drags me along. i am pulled through countless drunken, sweaty bodies and none of them even shiver at my presence.

what presence?

we go through a door next to the bar and descend down multiple sets of staircases. i'm reminded of my encounter with lamb back at the risqué cabaret. his office had also been behind the bar, through an ominous steel door. only here, at the casino, he seems to prefer the basement.

the boiler room.

a man screams behind the room's door. me #2 hesitates a moment, listening. someone's in agony. someone's pleading for a savior.

something tells me he isn't going to get one.

we walk through the door and find lamb and a couple others circling a man on the ground. tears and mucus and blood drips down the man's face and both present and past me look away, unable to process the grisly scene without wincing.

when we finally look back, lamb's smiling. he holds out his arms and says, 'well, it's about time.'

'sorry,' me #2 says. 'i was caught up in something.'

'and so—as you can see—am i.'

lamb kicks the man in the face and laughs at the repulsive sound he makes. the rest of the gang stares at the bloodbath, awaiting their turn.

'who's this?' me #2 asks.

'this?' lamb points at the man. 'this is a dead man. bobby, don't you know you're lookin' at a bona fide corpse right now?'

'what'd he do?'

lamb snorts and looks at his friends, who are also laughing like me #2's just told the funniest goddamn joke. 'i dunno,' lamb says, 'what did he do, kenny?'

the fattest one of the group spits on the man on the ground and says, 'this fool tried to straight up sabotage our whole motherfuckin' organization, yo.'

lamb bends down and grabs the man by the hair, yanking his head up to face me #2. 'we caught this little rodent trying to plant a fucking landmine under one of the craps tables. a landmine. can you fucking believe that, bobby?'

'refragatio,' me #2 whispers.

lamb nods. 'who else?'

'jesus christ,' me #2 says, stepping forward. 'you could have killed so many people. what the hell is wrong with you?'

the man spits out a glob of blood and says, 'i would have been doing them a favor. a thousand deaths is a fair price to pay in exchange for indigo's cocksucking head.'

a woman with bright, neon green hair leaps at him and bashes his nose open with a steel pipe.

'INDIGO IS A GOD, YOU FILTHY PEASANT!' the woman screams, hitting him over and over again. 'YOU ARE A LITTLE FLECK OF SHIT COMPARED TO

INDIGO'S GREATNESS. YOU FUCK. YOU STUPID FUCK. YOU ARE GOING TO DIE DOWN HERE, YOU'RE GOING TO FUCKING DIE, DON'T YOU REALIZE THAT?'

'ENOUGH!' lamb shouts, pulling her off him.

'let me finish him,' she pleads. 'let me feel the inside of his skull.'

'with a pipe?' lamb asks. 'nah, baby, that shit's too quick. don't you want to have a little fun?'

she pauses, staring at the man on the ground gagging on his own blood. 'yeah,' she says. 'i could use some fun right now.'

'why am i here?' me #2 asks. he looks pale and sick, like he's going to vomit.

'yeah,' kenny says, 'why the hell did you want him down here, anyway?'

lamb walks to us and puts an arm around me #2's shoulder. 'because, bobby here is still new. he hasn't exactly been properly introduced to our world. don't you all think it's about time we gave him that introduction?'

'what are you talking about?' me #2 says, shaking lamb's arm off him. 'i've been through the initiations. i've done what i was told.'

'yeah, but i ain't never seen you waste someone before,' lamb says, grinning.

'i don't need to waste anybody.'

'listen here, bobby-o,' lamb says. he walks toward the hostage on the ground and squats, staring at him. 'this world, this is a world of death. and until you embrace that death—boy, you ain't even livin'.'

'i don't want to kill him,' me #2 says. 'that isn't my fuckin' job, lamb.'

lamb stands up and spins toward us, his dreadlocks flinging in the air like wild snakes. 'your job is to obey the law of indigo, and this is what indigo wants. you wanna quit the family—already? bitch, you just started.'

surely he's not going to do it. please don't fucking do it.

'i don't even have a gun on me,' me #2 finally says, and lamb's smile widens.

'nah, man,' he says, 'if i'm not gonna let sonia use her pipe, why the hell would i allow a gun? hells nah, fuck that. we want to really make this little bitch squeal.'

me #2 doesn't answer, just looks down at the ground, avoiding eye contact.

everybody fades and becomes blurry for a moment, until me #2 lifts his head back up. lamb's standing in front of us, holding a large pot of water.

the water's boiling, steaming.

blistering.

'what do you want me to do with that?'

lamb shrugs, and a few drops of the water drops to the floor. it bubbles against the concrete. 'i don't know,' he says, 'i was just thinkin' our guest was lookin' a little thirsty, don't you think?'

'don't you think that's a bit much?' me #2 asks.

'it's nowhere near enough,' lamb says. 'but it'll do. plus, i've always wanted to see what would happen to someone if they drank a pot of boiling water. i bet it's gonna be pretty fuckin' cool.'

'hell yeah, now you're talkin',' the woman says, slapping her pipe against her palm.

'jesus,' me #2 whispers, taking the pot in his hands. he winces at the heat and fumbles to hold onto the handles. lamb steps away from us and everybody watches, licking their lips and waiting for the show to start.

the man on the ground trembles and whimpers at the sight of the pot and he realizes what's about to happen, and him and me both are praying to god it isn't actually going to.

'come on,' i say, staring at my past self. 'you can't fucking do this. this is crazy. you can't do this. if you can do this, then i can do this, and i sure as fuck don't want to be able to do this.'

but me #2 ignores my protests and steps forward,

staring at the man on the ground. the squirming refragatio.

'this is cruel,' me #2 finally says. 'i'm sorry, but i can't.'

the man on the ground reaches a shaking hand upward, blood pouring down his face. 'please,' he says, 'please, think of oasis, for the love of god, think of oasis.'

'what the fuck is he saying?' lamb asks.

me #2 doesn't hesitate. he shoves the pot of boiling water forward and pours it over the refragatio's face. the scream that follows is horrible. me #2 steps back, gasping at the man's face bubbling and oozing in front of him.

'oh my god,' me #2 says, staring, unable to look away.

what the fuck have we done?

lamb laughs. 'holy shit, look at that bitch's face. he's gonna explode!'

i try to look away, but my head's stuck in place, eyes frozen on the refragatio's bubbling flesh. me #2 still holds the pot of water, now barely half full. 'i'm sorry,' he whispers. 'i'm so sorry.'

the man on the ground reaches out again, and when he talks, it's barely audible. 'oh sis . . . oh sis . . .'

oasis.

('oasis. save oasis.')

'i'm sorry,' me #2 says again, and steps forward. he leans down and tilts the pot to the side, spilling the rest of the water into the refragatio's screaming mouth.

oh god.

no.

the boiler room throbs and pulsates and the bodies around me disintegrate into nonexistence. the room disappears, leaving me floating in absolute nothingness. my only companion is the sound of the man's scream stretching throughout all eternity.

chapter eighteen

Yeah. I know the Refragatio.
The Resistance.
Rebels.

The poor souls with enough balls to fight back against Indigo, to tell him he isn't shit. In the end, most of them suffer fates similar to the pot of boiling water. But then again, in the end, everybody eats a dirt sandwich. People on Indigo's bad side just don't get proper time to digest it.

"How do we reach the tunnels?" I ask Jed, finally taking him up on a second beer.

"There's a trap door here that'll lead to 'em. But don't even think about trying to find the Refragatio by yourself. You'll just get lost, place is a goddamn maze down there."

"How much to take us to them?" I ask, knowing that I don't have a dime to my name—or, at least if I do, I've forgotten about it. And I doubt Molly and the Rev have anything, either.

But, fortunately, Jed laughs and waves the thought away. "You can all pay me with the satisfaction of pissing off Indigo. Like I'd just let you lot get killed. I ain't no monster."

"Of course not," I say.

"Anyway," Jed says, "we can get into the tunnels from my toolshed out back. There's an entrance I've installed. But once we get down there, trust me, even with me as your guide it's going to be a hell of a trip. Very easy to get lost. I try not to go down there unless it's absolutely necessary."

"And the Refragatio, they'll be willing to help us?"

Jed smiles. "Yes, I think for you, they'll especially be willing."

"Well, what the hell does that mean?" Molly asks.

Ezzy erupts with a crying fit from the spare bedroom across the hallway.

"Shit," Molly says. "I thought she would have slept longer than that. Poor girl. I'll go take care of her."

I hold out my hand. "Let me."

"You sure?" she asks.

I nod. "I have some forgotten memories to remember."

In the bedroom, Ezzy's still crying under the blanket. She has it thrown over her tiny little body.

"Da-doo," she whimpers. "Da-doo, Da-doo."

"What's wrong, baby girl?" I ask, sitting down on the mattress. I slowly pull the blanket off her head. Tears stain her cheeks. She pushes her face against my hand, trying to get closer to me. I pick her up and hold her against my chest, letting her sit on my lap. "Everything's all right, I promise, it's okay."

"No, no," she says. "Not okay. *Not* okay."

"Yes it is, honey. Calm down."

"Bad, bad, bad. Bad." She points at the window over the nightstand, lips quivering. "Bad, bad, bad."

"Bad?" I ask, my stomach tightening.

"Bad."

"What kind of bad, baby?"

"Very bad."

I lay her back down on the mattress and stand up, leaning over the nightstand and peering through the window. Beyond the glass there is nothing but darkness. If I concentrate hard enough, I can see the outside of trees along the perimeter of the cabin's property. I lean closer, nearly pressing my face against the window, searching for . . . something. Something bad.

And something bad finds me.

Within the darkness, a white glow appears sudden and bright, like a candlewick giving birth to a flame.

A face, pale and deathly.

A smile, ancient and grotesque.

A harvey.

Its nostrils tense as it attempts to breathe us in through the glass, and its smile widens at the sound of my scream. I grab Ezzy off the mattress and sprint out of the bedroom, slamming the door behind me and running into the kitchen. I stop cold at the sight of a dozen armed gunmen, pointing their weapons at myself and everybody else. Lamb stands at the lead of the gunmen, his dreadlocks hanging over his face. His jaw's bandaged and stained with blood. Jesus Christ, how can he still be alive?

"Hey Bobby," the Rev says. "You recognize this fucker?"

"Yeah," I say. "I put a bullet in his face not too long ago."

"No, no, not that cunt. The other cunt." He points at a dirty, raggedly looking man holding a snubnose pistol. "He was the bloke at the mono station, the one with newspapers for drawers. Motherfucker snitched."

"Shut your faces, sinners!" the gunman says. "You'll all pay for going against the word of Conundrae."

"Shit," I say.

"Shit, is right," Lamb says. When he talks, I can hear the strain in his voice. Every syllable must be a bitch to pronounce.

"How are you still alive?" I ask him.

"Funny," Lamb says. "Last night, I was the one asking *you* that question."

"Hell," I say. "We're all just full of mysteries, aren't we?"

I look down at the kitchen table. Jed's face is covered in blood, but he's still alive, still breathing. Someone must've whacked him something fierce. Molly's just sitting at the end of the table, shaking, eyes glued on our daughter. I hold Ezzy close against my chest, not knowing where this is going, but knowing it isn't going anywhere good.

"Ow, Da-doo," Ezzy says, and I realize I'm holding her a bit too tight.

Remarkably, all his goons look near identical, like carbon copies of Raoul. Somehow I doubt my abilities in taking them all down as I had the last group. For one thing, I'm fresh out of vibrators. I try to concentrate on my mind powers instead, but the strain just inflicts a migraine.

"Where do you get all those guys?" I ask, as Lamb nears. "The Big Dumb Bad Guy Warehouse?"

"There's a staffing agency," Lamb explains. He holds up his gun and jams it into my face. "I don't know how the hell you keep getting away, but there won't be no repeat this time, motherfucker."

Ezzy reaches up and wraps her tiny fingers around the huge barrel of his gun. She giggles at the coldness.

"Well, hello," Lamb says, eyes looking down. "What're you doing, little girl?"

"Fuck off," I whisper, and he knees me in the gut, making me double over with a very audible grunt. Lamb snatches Ezzy from my arms.

"I'll take that," he says gleefully, and brings down the handle of his gun into the back of my skull. My face meets the floor.

"No, Da-doo, no!" Ezzy cries.

I look up just in time to see Molly charging at Lamb, only to be elbowed in the face by one of his goons. She falls down next to me. The Rev starts to stand up from the table, but sits back down after another goon shoves a gun in his face.

Ezzy screams, howls. "No, no, no!" She smacks Lamb in the face repeatedly.

"Dammit, girl," Lamb says, "I've punched a baby before, don't think I won't do it again."

He hands her to one of his Raoul-looking goons. "Take her, will you? Indigo might be interested in her, see what he says. Not every day we can offer Conundrae a fresh baby."

"Yes, boss." Two of them go out the kitchen exit, one carrying Ezzy. She screams for me to help.

"No!" I shout, attempting to get up. I am put right back down by another pistol-whipping from Lamb. Molly doesn't seem to move—the elbow to the face must have knocked her out cold.

I watch the man walk away with my little girl.

No.

I sit up and stare at their backs, burying my vision within their flesh. I visualize their skeletons ripping apart and turning to dust. I visualize—

"Oh, no, I don't think so, motherfucker," Lamb says, and shoots me in the chest.

And then all I can understand is pain.

Ezzy's cries fade in the distance.

Everything fades.

Life fades.

Ezzy . . .

I've failed.

No . . . god, no . . .

chapter nineteen

Something's wrong. I'm not dead.

The pain's too strong to open my eyes, but at least I can actually feel pain, instead of the alternative. Instead of nothing.

My chest feels like it's on fire. Everything's in pieces and I wither on the floor, screaming. I hear Molly and Ezzy screaming my name, but I can't acknowledge them, can't even fucking look at them.

The insides of my chest seem to be moving around, like loose flecks of dirt in the wind. Everything is warm, everything is hot. Everything is miserable. But, somehow, I am not dead, and I can't forget that. Forgetting that means forgetting how to breathe, forgetting how to function.

I need to function if I'm going to save Ezzy.

And I must save Ezzy.

I try to sit up, but my body doesn't budge. All my energy's concentrated on my chest—no, not just my chest, but my heart. That motherfucker, *he shot me in the heart.*

How am I still alive?

What is happening to me?

I think about the harvey in the window. I think about my powers. My weird, stubborn abilities. They don't come when I want them to, but when *they* feel like it. And right now, they certainly feel like it.

I think about what Jed had said.

("With a harvey, life continues, even if the organ in

question is no longer connected to where it's supposed to be connected.")

And I realize that the sensation in my chest isn't in my head: there really is something moving around. My literal broken heart's being sewn back together. Holy shit. The power is in my mind. The life force is my brain, and whatever's hiding inside it.

How many spiders are in me right now, working me raw like a perpetual motion machine?

Slowly but surely, sugar pie.

That voice again. Who does it belong to?

"Bobby! Oh, god, Bobby, wake up!"

I open my eyes. Molly's kneeling over me, sobbing on my face.

"I think I'm good," I say, and she gasps and kisses me.

It doesn't last long.

Lamb kicks her off of me and gives me a curious look. "Well, how the fuck is that fair?"

My skull feels like an empty, metal bucket, and there's a crazy person inside of it swinging an aluminum baseball bat against the walls. Gritting through bloody teeth, I say, "Your bullets are mosquito bites."

I spit at him. He just stands there, still, the spit trickling down his cheek.

He raises his gun, then gasps. His legs collapse and he falls to the floor beside me, motionless.

A large steak knife sticks out of his back.

I look up. Molly's standing above us, breathing heavily, crying.

"Nice one," I tell her.

"Let's go," she says.

"Good idea."

The Rev helps me to my feet. All of Lamb's men are gone. "Where the hell did everybody go?"

"He had them search the premises," Jed says. "They're trying to find my entrance to the tunnels."

"What should we do then?" Molly asks. "Those bastards have my daughter."

"She's probably gone by now."

"*What?*"

"I mean, the people who took her have gained too much distance. We won't catch up to them on foot."

"Well, where would they take her?" I ask.

Jed stares at me and waits for me to answer my own question.

"The casino?" I guess.

"Indigo almost never leaves the building. Of course they're taking her to the casino."

"Well, that's where we have to go then."

Jed nods. "Agreed, but first, we have a small army outside ready to tear us apart. We need to be able to defend ourselves."

"And how do you suppose we do that?" Molly asks.

And Jed grins.

Jed leads us out of the kitchen and down the hallway to the master bedroom.

The Rev takes one look at the king size bed and says, "Mate, now is not the time for a nap."

Jed grunts and nods to the opposite site of the bedroom. "This way."

He opens a door and pushes us into a walk-in closet, shutting the door behind us.

"We can't just stay here and hide," Molly says. "We have to find Ezzy."

"We're not hiding," Jed says. He sounds distracted, preoccupied. "Just hold on a second, will ya?"

"Unless you have Narnia hiding back here, this plan is terrible," the Rev says.

In the darkness of the closet, someone knocks on the wall. An instant later the closet wall slides open, revealing a brightly lit room beyond the hanging coats.

"Holy shit," the Rev says. "You *do* have Narnia."

We enter the secret room and our eyes glue themselves to the walls. Various weapons hang from floor to ceiling: pistols, shotguns, machineguns, rifles, chainsaws, samurai swords, the works.

"Welcome to the barracks," Jed says, limping toward the guns. He gives Molly a small pistol and tells her how to use it. He nods at us. "Get something and make sure it's loaded. We've still a long way to go."

The Rev's eyes glow as he zones in on a shotgun. "Oh, hell yes."

I grab a machinegun since it's the closest thing within reach. Every one of these things can kill. There's no reason to be picky. Jed takes a machinegun of his own and collects extra ammo and shells for our weapons, distributing them to the group.

"You guys ready for this?" he asks.

"No," Molly says.

Voices erupt from the master bedroom: "They're in the closet!"

"Oh crap," Jed says, and sprints across the barracks. He slams his fist against a red button and the secret passageway slides shut just as a round of bullets bursts through the closet.

"It's all right," Jed says. "The entire room is strong enough to withstand a nuclear bomb."

"Somehow I doubt that," I say. "What do we do now?"

He shrugs. "Sit and wait, I suppose."

"Man, fuck that shit," the Rev says, rocking up and down on his toes. "Let's go kick their asses!"

"Are you insane?" Molly says. "As soon as we open the door, they'll shoot our faces off."

We stand there, holding our weapons and listening to the men in the other room shoot at us. The gunfire is muffled by the walls, making it almost sound like we're underwater.

"Well," Jed finally says, "we could always just blow them up."

172

He moves across the room and pulls a hand grenade off the wall. He holds it up to us like a trophy. "This will shut them up a bit, yeah?"

I nod. "Yeah."

The Rev pulls another grenade from the wall and sticks it in his pants. When he notices me watching him, he shrugs. "Hey, we might need one later."

"You're gonna end up blowing your dick off."

He shrugs again. "I've had worse things happen to it."

"Anyway," Jed says, "it's probably a good idea if y'all get to the other side of the room. This ain't gonna be pretty."

Jed leans his ear against the wall, listening. Then he opens the door again, pulls the pin off the grenade, and tosses the grenade through the coats, into the bedroom.

"Hey, they're not dead!" one of the men shout.

Jed closes the door again just as the bedroom explodes. The barracks shakes for a moment, then goes still. The men are no longer shooting.

"All right," Jed says. "The goal is to get to the toolshed. There's a small crawlspace opening behind it—we go through that, we get to the tunnels. Best way to the toolshed is through the door in the kitchen. You guys ready?"

Yeah. We're ready. We have to be. Every second we aren't moving onward is another second Ezzy's not in my arms.

The time to move is now.

The bedroom is destroyed. Half the ceiling has collapsed into the room. Blood stains the floor, sticking to our feet as we pass through. We exit the bedroom and move down the hallway, toward the kitchen. Jed holds up his hand and indicates for us to stop until he confirms the coast is clear. He peeks his head into the kitchen doorway and immediately pulls back seconds before a round of gunfire bursts past.

"Shit, how many are there?" I ask.

"Two, maybe three."

"We're screwed," the Rev says. "I don't even know how to use a shotgun."

"How thick are these walls?" I ask.

Jed shrugs. "Not very." He realizes what I'm thinking, and nods. "Let's do it."

"You go ahead," I tell him, kneeling down by the doorway.

Jed presses the muzzle of his machinegun against the wall and holds down the trigger, blindly releasing a spray of bullets.

Ignoring the pain in my chest, I leap into the kitchen and dive over the table, tackling one of the gunmen as he shields himself from Jed's bullets. Amazingly, I manage to dodge the bullets as well.

I slam the butt of my gun into the man's skull and he stops struggling. Another smack to the head and he's completely limp—either unconscious or simply dead, I don't care which. Ahead of me another one has realized what I'm doing, and he's fumbling for his own gun. I unleash a round of bullets into his chest before he even has time to aim.

Another one screams behind me as he rises from cover, raising his own machinegun toward me. The Rev's shotgun goes off from across the room, and the man about to shoot me suddenly suffers from exploding head syndrome.

"Holy shit," the Rev says, looking at the shotgun, then back at the headless goon. "That was gross."

I manage to stand up and slap him on the shoulder. "Thanks, man," I say. "You just saved my life."

"Like it's the first time," the Rev says. His face's pale and sick as he stares at the gore decorating the kitchen. "You can repay the favor by making sure nobody ever shoots me. That seems like it would *really* hurt." A gun goes off behind us, and the Rev shouts, "Ugh! Someone shot me!" Then he collapses.

I don't think. I react.

My vision narrows in on the goon shooting at me. The bullets disintegrate to ash before they even reach their destination. The guy's eyes widen in horror as an invisible gust of wind punches him in the chest and sends him flying against the wall. The sound of his back snapping in half is loud and permanent.

For a moment, my chest is an inferno. Flecks of my heart fall apart. I take a deep breath, focusing on putting myself back together. A moment later, I'm able to breathe without it hurting again.

I look down at the Rev. He's lying there, crying. Molly and Jed slowly enter the kitchen, guns aimed and ready to blow somebody away. A little too late, though.

"Holy balls," Molly gasps. "Rev got shot!"

"He's fine," I say. "It's only his ass. He'll live."

"No I won't!" the Rev cries. "My arse! My beautiful *arrssse!*"

"Oh, shut up," I say. "Hey, did you see what I did?"

"What are you talking about?"

"I did it. The telekinesis."

"You didn't do shit," the Rev says, using the edge of the sink to pull himself to his feet.

"Stop bickering, we got to go," Jed says. "Who knows how many of these bastards are left."

"Hey, wait," Molly says, staring at the floor. "Where's Lamb?"

She's right. He's gone. Shit.

"He can't be too far," I tell her. "Guy has to be bleeding out. You stabbed him pretty good."

"Just keep your eyes out," Jed says, leading us through the kitchen. The cabinets have all fallen to the floor and shattered, either from the goons searching the place or from the grenade. We go through the backdoor one at a time, slowly, expecting to find a thousand more gunmen outside waiting for us.

We don't find any gunmen, but we don't find nothing, either.

175

The night is no longer so dark. Up ahead, between us and the toolshed, a cloud of white floats. No, not a cloud. Three creatures, three pale mysterious beings.

"What the fuck is that?" the Rev asks, gripping his shotgun tighter.

"Harvies," I say.

"They're beautiful," Molly says.

"I've never been so close to one before," Jed says. "I don't know what to do."

"I guess we should shoot them." The Rev raises the shotgun, but before he can pull the trigger, he's knocked off his feet and thrown across the yard.

"Shit," Jed says, and raises his own weapon. His arm freezes halfway up, and his body goes still. We all go still. I try to move, but I'm locked in place. The harvies stare at us and slowly glide closer. Underneath their surgical masks, I know they're smiling. *Snarling*.

The three harvies surround Jed, leaning over him, breathing him in. Molly and I are helpless, trapped. I watch them circle Jed from my peripheral vision. Jed grunts, moans.

"Ah, damn," Jed says, and howls in agony.

"Stop!" I scream, but the rest of my body refuses to move.

The sound of bones shattering silences his screaming, and Jed collapses, broken from their death gaze and free to decompose in peace. And I know without even having to look that they've cracked his sternum. Not only that, but they've pulled his goddamn heart out.

This is what they're going to do to all of us, I realize. One by one, they'll take our hearts and deliver them to Indigo.

With Jed out of the picture, the three harvies move to the next person in line: Molly. She whimpers as they sniff in her scents. Any moment they'll rip out her fucking heart. She knows it, I know it, *they* know it.

But fuck that.

And fuck them.

This time, when I try to move, I don't just try. I *do*. I turn my head to the side, forcing my body through a strong, phantom current of wind. They don't notice at first that I've broken their spell, but they start to pay attention when their pale, milky white skin begins flaking off their faces. They release their grip on Molly and turn toward me, making a disgusting hissing sound through their surgical masks. I feel my heart chipping away, piece by piece, but I fight through it and concentrate every ounce of energy on ripping these harvies a new asshole.

I refuse to blink. Blinking means defeat. I stare, wide-eyed, mouth in mid-scream, sending enough power to fuel a tsunami into their rotting, spider-infested minds. I don't know how long we stay like this. It feels like days, but realistically, probably just a few seconds.

The harvies howl something wicked and their bodies explode simultaneously, leaving behind a cluster of tiny black spiders. They scurry away in the grass, toward the forest, in search of new hosts to consume. The world spins and I feel my eyeballs rolling into my skull, and I'm falling to the ground, my body weight greater than the density of a dying sun.

When I reawaken, Molly's on top of me, crying and begging me not to be dead. I start coughing, and my chest is still spinning, trying to stitch itself back together. I hadn't passed out. No. I think I literally died. But whatever's inside of me, it's not giving up that easily. Even when I'm dead, it'll still fight.

The bullet Lamb put through my heart, it's going to be affecting me for the rest of my life. Every time I try to use my telekinesis on something else, I'll no longer be focusing my energy on keeping my heart in one piece. So, basically, if I'm going to use these mind powers, it better be fucking worth it.

"Are you okay?" Molly asks.

"No," I tell her. "But that doesn't matter."

I force myself to sit up, then climb to my feet. Everything is still spinning and I feel like I'm one violent cough away from ripping my chest in half. But Molly's next to me, holding my hand, telling me how much she loves me and how she thought I was dead. I hold off telling her I *was* dead. I don't think she would be able handle it. Shit, I can't even handle it.

I refuse to look down at Jed, because I know if I do, I'll see what the inside of his chest looks like. I save the memories of before the ambush and throw away everything else. Jed saved us. He gave us shelter, food, lodging. He was going to deliver us to safety. He died helping us. For that, I'll be forever grateful.

"Oy!" the Rev shouts from behind us. "Look who I found!"

We turn around. The Rev's stumbling toward us, dragging Lamb by his feet through the grass. His body squirms as he attempts to break free, but he's too weak to cause any real damage. The steak knife still sticks out of his back. When the Rev stops next to us, he bends down and pulls the knife out, and Lamb screams.

"You're all a bunch of bitches!" Lamb shouts. "Every last one of you! *Bitches!*"

"How are you even still talking?" I ask. "I thought I shot your jaw off."

"Not all of it, motherfucker."

"Well, I'm sorry, then," I say. "I guess I don't have the best aim."

"What do you think we should do with him, Bobby?" the Rev asks. He holds up the steak knife, indicating for me to stab him a few more times.

"Just shoot the fucker and let's get out of here," Molly says. "We have to find Ezzy."

"Which is exactly why we need him alive," I say. "We're going to use him."

"How?" Molly asks.

"We're going to trade him to the Refragatio in exchange for leading us to Indigo's casino."

"Do you think they'd want him?"

I stare down at him and think about boiling pots of water. "Yeah," I say, "they'll want him."

Molly touches my cheek and looks deep into my eyes. She's crying, and so am I.

"Is Ezzy going to be okay?" she asks.

And I know she doesn't want this kind of answer, but it's the only answer I can give her:

"I don't know."

iii.
everything you
ever knew

chapter twenty

One by one, we crawl under the toolshed and climb down a long ladder leading into the tunnels. Before I follow the rest of them, I push Lamb down and smile at the sound of him briefly screaming and then landing roughly below. The odor makes us gag: it's a combination of shit and vomit and then more shit. I get the feeling that if there was actually any lighting down here, we'd see many rotting animal carcasses.

"Stand up," I tell Lamb.

"Suck my balls."

I shove the gun in his face, and he decides to stand up after all. I grip on to his dreadlocks and push him forward, the muzzle of the gun nestling comfortably against his spine. If I let go of him for even a second, I'll lose him in the darkness.

"I don't suppose anybody thought to bring a flashlight," Molly says.

I sigh. "Let's just move forward. Molly, keep your hand on my back, and Rev, keep your hand on Molly."

"With pleasure," the Rev says.

"I can easily shoot your other ass cheek. Don't forget that."

"Point taken."

"What's the plan, then?" Molly asks. "Just keep walking until something happens?"

"Bingo," I say.

"We're all going to die in these tunnels," Lamb says.

"The only shit we'll find down here is our own nonexistence."

We push onward into total darkness. Once in a while we walk into a wall and take it as a sign to turn left or right. Anything could be here in the tunnels with us, slithering along the floors and ceilings, preparing to attack. But nothing tries to eat us, so we continue. Lamb attempts to talk more, but shuts up once I tap his knife wound with the machinegun.

"Man, we're not gonna find this place," the Rev says. "We don't even know *what place* we're looking for. We're fucked."

"We don't have any other choice," I say.

"I'm sick of walking. My arse is killing me. Shit, it might literally be killing me. What if I'm bleeding to death?"

"You'll live."

"Easy for you to say. You have the anti-bullet powers. What do I got?"

"A cute Mohawk," I say.

"Just admit that we're screwed. Jed said that even he had trouble finding their hideout, and he'd *been there* before. What does that mean for us?"

"It means we keep moving."

"This is bullshit, man," the Rev says. "It's not like we're just gonna suddenly stumble across it. Something like this is top secret, yeah? It's not gonna be as simple as turning another corner and walking right into it."

We turn another corner and walk right into it.

"Oh," the Rev says. "Well, never mind then."

The tunnel's wall breaks off into an expansive opening. There are hundreds of candles scattered about this space, devouring the darkness and revealing all the faces of its inhabitants. There are dozens of people here, sitting on couches, playing ping pong, sleeping on mattresses, reading books. The majority of them wear little to no clothing for reasons that continue to baffle me.

Their heads turn toward us as we approach.

We stop, frozen. A part of me anticipates a bullet to the head. We don't know these people. We're strangers in their eyes, and we just walked into their home.

I slowly wave at them and say, "Uh, hi."

"Yo!" the Rev says.

"Fuck," Lamb says.

Some of them nod, a few grunt, and then they return to what they were doing.

A bulky man approaches the end of the station and indicates for us not to come any closer. He waves a machete at us.

"The fuck are you?"

"Well," I say, nodding at my hostage, "this is Jason Lamb, and I have a feeling you two might have a lot to talk about."

The man gasps at his name. "Lamb?"

I nod again. "Yup."

The man looks at his machete, then at Lamb, then back to his machete. He smiles.

"Fuck," Lamb says.

The man gestures at the rest of us. "And who are you?"

"I'm Bobby, this is Molly, and this is . . . uh, the Rev, I guess."

The Rev bows, then says, "Is this like a nudist camp or something? Because this is awesome."

"I apologize for anything he says," Molly says. "He's actually been shot, and we were hoping you might be able to help patch him up."

The man nods. "Of course, ma'am. Right this way. By the way, my name is Samuel."

He leads us through the hideout and motions for the Rev to lay down on a dirty, bloodstained mattress. He snaps his fingers at a woman sitting on a sofa, reading a magazine about motorcycles called *Vroom! Vroom!*. "Aggie!" he shouts. "This man needs help, he's been shot." He turns to the Rev. "Where were you shot?"

"My arse."

"Gross." He turns back to the woman. "He's been shot in the ass. Take care of him."

The woman nods and gets up, grabs a first aid kit from the wall and attends to the Rev.

"Finally," he says. "I'm only bleeding to death here."

"You guys go ahead and have a seat. I'll go find Mercedes. She'll want to meet you." He looks at Lamb and smiles. "Especially you."

"I can't wait," Lamb says.

We all sit down on these foldable chairs that smell like trash, but at least they're somewhat comfortable. I guide Lamb to sit on the floor beside me, and I keep the machinegun pressed against the back of his skull.

"You know, this ain't gonna end well for any of us," Lamb says. "I might die right now, and that's okay. But you? Boy, you are gonna suffer a fate worse than anybody. Conundrae is gonna personally shit in your mouth, son. You ready for that?"

"Hmm," I say. "I suppose so."

Samuel rounds up some food and water for us all and tells us Mercedes is on her way. I don't pretend to understand what is in the bowls he hands us: it's some kind of thick liquid, almost like oatmeal. It smells horrible, but tastes pretty okay. We eat it like we haven't eaten in ages.

The Rev curses the woman fixing his wounds.

"Quit being a pussy," Molly says.

"You try getting shot in the arse!"

"I know I'd at least have some balls about it," she says. "Jesus."

The Rev chooses to not say anything and closes his eyes, wincing at the medicine the woman pours over his opened wound.

Samuel returns with another woman at his side. The woman, who I take to be named Mercedes, stares at me like we know each other. Then she looks at Lamb and laughs.

"You always said one day you'd bring Lamb down here. And now you have. Color me impressed."

Molly turns toward me. "Do you, uh, know this woman?"

"I . . . I don't know."

Mercedes shakes her head slowly. "It must be terrifying, to lose your memory. I can't even imagine."

"I'm making do," I tell her.

Mercedes looks down at Lamb again. "What, oh what, are we going to do with you?"

"I guess you could suck my cock?" he suggests, and Mercedes laughs for a good couple seconds before lifting up her foot and driving it into his face. He falls down on his back, either unconscious or dead. Blood streams out of his face, as if she kicked his nose into his brain.

"Well, now that he's out of the way, we can really talk," she says. "So tell me, where's that beautiful daughter of yours?"

"They took her," I whisper, trying to ignore Molly's sudden whimpering. "That's why we came here. We need your help. We have to get her back."

"The casino?"

"Can't you take me there?

Mercedes nods. "Yeah, there's a path. If your memory wasn't so wonky, you'd remember taking it."

"Well, that's the point: I don't remember, but you do."

"And do you know who I am?" she asks.

"Someone named Mercedes. You're connected with the Refragatio. According to Jed, you can help us. You're the *only* people who can help us."

"You've talked to Jed? Where is he?"

I don't respond, I just stare at her, unable to say what needs to be said. But it's enough. She lowers her head, redirecting her vision to her feet. "Goddamn them. Goddamn them all." A moment passes, and she clears her throat. "All right, there's nothing we can do about Jed now. But there's a chance we can still save your baby. So let's focus on her instead."

"Thank you," Molly says.

I reach over and hold Molly's hand. She squeezes it back.

Lamb begins stirring back awake and Mercedes stomps his face again. She sits at the table with us, thinking for a moment, then says, "Look, there's this grate in the casino's laundry room. It leads into the tunnels, which lead to these tunnels. It's the way you've traveled from here to there and there to here in the past."

"That sounds perfect," I say.

"Yeah, the only thing is," Mercedes says, "the room is really small, there's no way we could all come in that way undetected. Because, let's face it, one person isn't going to defeat Indigo alone, so you *do* need us. And we need you. It's about time we rose and took care of this tyrant once and for all. With Jed's passing . . . " She wipes a tear from her eye. "No, the time to wait is over, and the time to act is now."

"I'm glad we're on the same page, then."

"If we all came in through the laundry room, it would be a bloodbath. But I've been thinking, and my theory is: Indigo doesn't want you dead."

I laugh. "Of course he wants me dead. That's the whole reason I got stuck in this mess. The asshole tried to kill me."

"Yeah, but you didn't die, now did you? Indigo never makes a mistake, yet here you are. He has to be curious. Wouldn't you be? I'm betting anything he wants to perform further experiments on you. Something, you know? He's a scientist. He would be a fool to simply execute you. So that's why my thought is: what if you go up there first, alone, and seek out Indigo yourself? I mean, I doubt you'll succeed, but even if you're caught, they aren't going to kill you right away."

Molly shakes her head. "I don't like this idea all of a sudden."

I sit back up, nodding. It makes sense. "And with me caught, the guards will be distracted."

Mercedes smiles. "Giving us an opportune time to come in through the front doors, taking back what's ours, one machete at a time."

"That's crazy!" Molly says.

"Of course it is," I say. "It's fucking nuts."

Mercedes says, "So, you agree then?"

"Hell yeah."

"Bobby!" Molly cries.

I look at her and grab her hand, trying to smile. "This could be our only chance to save her."

She doesn't say anything, just pleads at me with her eyes for an alternative solution that doesn't exist.

"Now listen," Mercedes says, "there are some things you still need to be reminded of. We've been watching this city go to hell for a long time now. The cause of it, as you can imagine, is Indigo. This man, this cult leader, came in one day and ruined it all. He's a con artist who created his own religion to get rich."

"How is that any different than other religions?" the Rev pipes in, then yelps as the woman continues to stitch him up.

Mercedes continues, "He came up with this very stupid idea about a demon he calls *Conundrae*. According to him, this demon feasts upon the organs of humans."

I recall the contents of that cooler. The heart. Jesus Christ.

"Those who join his cult have to help feed this demon," Mercedes says. "Supposedly, it's their way of buying their own paradise once *Conundrae* is summoned up and begins turning humanity into its own personal slaves."

I pause, trying not to vomit in my mouth, then say, "I've seen the organs. This guy at a drugstore tried giving me somebody's heart."

Mercedes nods. "Right, I'm not saying they don't deal with organs. But not for the reasons that Indigo claims. In really, he's probably just selling them on the black market. That's how he's managed to become so wealthy, so fast. It's why he has his own casino now—a casino that serves as a haven for booze and drugs. Not to mention the death fights."

"Death fights," I echo.

"Go there any night, you'll find a cage in the middle of the bar. There's always a fight going on. Only one person can leave the cage alive. Half the time, they're slaves being forced to fight. It's despicable."

"Goddamn."

"I know," Mercedes says. "That isn't the worst part, sadly. I wish it was. But Indigo also has this machine. I've never seen it, none of us have, but we've heard about it. It's locked away somewhere in the casino. He uses it to reprogram people. Erases their memories, turns their souls inside-out. That's how he makes his spooky fucking ghosts."

I nod. "His own personal organ harvesters."

"Correct," Mercedes says, face caught in a grimace. "These . . . harvies, they normally have no will of their own. They become puppets. But sometimes, the procedure, I guess it doesn't go too well, and the harvey leaves with some sense of who they once were. It's complicated shit and half of this comes from secondhand rumors, but there's gotta be some truth to it. I mean—look at you."

I feel countless eyes on me, prying my brain apart. "How do we know each other, exactly?" I ask her.

Mercedes laughs. "You still don't remember, do you?"

"I don't . . . "

"Just wait," she says. "It'll come to you. You have to be patient, Detective Oasis."

"Excuse me?" Molly says.

But I'm already gone.

(interlude vi)

me #2 is sitting in front of a huge oak desk, and behind it is a bald man with a mustache, wearing a suit. me #2 looks like he's somewhere in his early twenties. he embodies innocence. his eyes show hope for the future. i'm standing at the side of the desk, watching them talk. i can't get past the image of how me #2 is wearing a police cadet uniform, and how surprisingly good i look in it.

suddenly everything comes back to me.

the bald man is saying, 'you understand what this all means, correct?'

me #2 nods. remains silent.

'life as you know it will cease to be,' the bald man says. 'you will no longer be an employee of the police department. your files will be erased. your brother, even though he is also an officer, will no longer be an acquaintance of any kind. if you see him on the street, you do not see him as family. you see him as an enemy. he is one of the few who have been informed of this operation, and he knows the repercussions for blowing your cover. he will not blow your cover. you will not blow your cover."

'yes, sir,' me #2 says.

'you will no longer say "yes, sir". you are not well-mannered. in fact, you are scum. you will blend in with the rest of the delinquents that run this city. you will begin from the very bottom, and you will work your way up. you understand that you will be forced to do crimes against society, crimes against humanity?'

'yes, sir.'

'and you are willing to do such things in order to ensure your mission is carried out successfully?'

'yes, sir.'

the bald man raises his eyebrow at him. at me. 'what did i say about the "yes, sir" crap?'

me #2 pauses, clears his throat, and says, 'all right, bitch, whatever you fuckin' say.'

the bald man nods approvingly. 'you will take a new name. it doesn't matter, odds are they will assign you a name again once you infiltrate the cult. you will do as they say. you must not jeopardize your cover. if they discover who you are, you won't just be killed. you will be tortured to the fullest extent of their sick and twisted imaginations. you must carry out the mission.'

'i will.'

'what is the mission?'

'to bring down indigo,' me #2 says.

'at all costs,' the bald man adds.

'at all costs.'

'i will contact you when needed. you do not ever attempt to contact me or anyone else in the department. understood?'

'understood.'

'good,' the bald man says. 'now get the fuck out of my office and go save the world.'

'suck my dick, pig,' me #2 says, and shakes the bald man's hand.

this is insane. this is total lunacy. i'm a cop. i've always been a cop. holy shit, what the hell have i gotten into?

i follow me #2 out of the office and into the hallway. there's another officer waiting for us. i recognize him instantly. it's the same guy i found at the river.

the one i killed.

'hey, bro,' detective oasis says.

me #2 nods. 'hey.'

'so this is it,' oasis says.

'looks like it.'

'you know, i don't like this.'

'i know,' me #2 says.

'but it's what has to be done.'

'yeah.'

'i'm going to be checking on you every chance i get. pulling you over for bogus speeding violations, planting heroin on you and stuff.'

'i wouldn't expect anything less.'

a tear drips down oasis's cheek. 'you just be glad ma isn't here for this. she'd go berserk.'

me #2 laughs. 'she would make you really arrest me just so i'd be out of danger.'

oasis says, 'yeah, i'd have to go shoot some idiot and hide the gun in your trunk.'

there's a moment where they just stand there, not saying anything, taking it all in.

'just do as i said. find mercedes. she already knows the score. she's probably the only person who will be able to help you from here on.'

'i'll find her.'

oasis says, 'i love you, you know.'

'i love you too, marv.'

oasis wraps his arms around me #2, hugging him tight against his chest. 'if you die out there,' he says, 'i swear to god i'll kill you.'

brothers. me and oasis, we're brothers. i'm a fucking cop and my brother is one, too.

my brother, who is dead.

dead because of me.

i killed him.

my own fucking brother.

jesus christ. no.

the hallway begins to shake violently while the light fixtures flicker. yet nobody notices but me. a loud sucking sound follows, and my spirit is vacuumed from the mind trip and back into reality, where i no longer wish to exist.

me, a cop.
dead, my brother.
fuck me.

chapter twenty-one

"**A** COP? A fucking *cop?*"

Molly looks mad. I don't blame her. She smacks me across the face and I let her. Mostly because I'm pretty sure she can take me in a fight, if push comes to shove.

"You bastard, you lousy *bastard,*" she says, expecting some kind of retaliation.

But I just sit there, face stinging from Molly's hand. "It's true," I whisper. "I remember it all. I'm sorry, but it's true."

"I knew," the Rev says, still lying down with his eyes closed as the woman fixes his wounds. "You told me a long time ago one night when we were both wasted."

Well, that I certainly don't remember.

Molly screams, "*You* knew?" She looks at me and slaps me again. "You told *him* but you didn't tell *me?* I'm your goddamn girlfriend for Christ's sake! We have a *child* together, and you don't think it's a good idea to tell me you're a fucking undercover cop? Jesus fucking Christ, Bobby. Or whatever the hell your name is."

"I don't know," I say quietly, and I truly don't. I don't know what kind of person I even am. Someone who can go years and years lying to the one he loves most. Molly's right. How could I have had a child with this woman without letting her know who I really am?

Molly snaps back at the Rev. "Why didn't you say anything?"

The Rev shrugs. "Yeah, I probably should have mentioned something. Guess I didn't really think about it."

"How could you *not* think about it?"

"I don't know! I thought it would be rude to bring it up."

"You're such an idiot," Molly says.

"What does that have to do with anything?"

"Enough!" I shout, making them both jump back, startled. I stand up, drenched in sweat. "The truth is, I guess I'm a cop. But what does that change? Yes, I've lied, and I've been a horrible human being to you all. But there's still one undeniable truth that cannot be changed right now, and that is Indigo—that *fuck*, he has our daughter. And we aren't doing her any good by sitting around here arguing."

But Molly isn't letting this drop so easily. "Everything I know about you is a lie. Why have I even been helping you? I don't even know who *you* are. It's because of *you* that Ezzy is missing. *You*, you lying coward of a man."

I grab her cheeks and move my face close to hers, so our noses are touching. "I'm sorry," I whisper. "I know it's all my fault. She's gone because of me. Your life is fucked because of me. But I'm going to fix it, I promise, Mol, it'll be okay. I *will* get our daughter back. She will be safe."

"Why should I believe you?" Molly asks.

And I don't have any lines of comfort. I'm not the hero I want to be. I'm not anything. So I tell her the truth.

"I don't know," I tell her, "but you should."

Molly smiles weakly.

We kiss. I try to ignore the hesitation on her end. Whatever we once had, it's damaged now—possibly beyond repair.

"We should get moving," Mercedes says. "There's a little girl who needs to get back to her family."

Molly stays behind with the Rev, who eventually passed out from the pain in his ass. Before we leave, we come up with a plan of attack. As I'm infiltrating the casino via the laundry room, the rest of the Refragatio will be busy hijacking the monorail and riding it toward the station closest to the casino. They'll rig it to stay at the station while they storm the entrance of the casino, and once Indigo's dead, we'll make our escape on the mono.

I wish Molly had come with us, though. At least, just for the walk. I can use her company right now. She doesn't trust me now. I don't blame her. I don't trust me, either.

It's just me and Mercedes walking through the darkened tunnels. Every once in a while, she flicks on her lighter to determine where we are, but she's traveled through these tunnels enough to not need light. She does it for my benefit.

"Let's be honest," I say.

"All right."

"Do you think he's killed Ezzy?"

"I don't know," she says. "I doubt it. If Indigo knows that you defeated the last wave of his henchmen, then he'll keep her alive as incentive for you to come back to claim her. He's expecting you right now, I'm sure of it. This will be a trap that you're walking right into, but we don't have any other choice."

"I know."

"Your best bet is to carry on like you aren't anticipating the trap. Because if you get caught too easily, then Indigo is going to know something is up, and put his guards on extra alert. Which means when we come in the front entrance, we'll all be screwed. We won't stand a chance."

Our feet splash in puddles of shit-water. My funny bunnies are ruined. I remind myself that Mercedes is barefoot right now. My face makes a grimace that I'm glad she can't see.

"And what exactly are you guys going to do once you get in?" I ask.

"We're going to kill them," Mercedes answers calmly. "We're going to kill them all."

"Will you make sure Molly stays behind, when it all goes down? I don't want her involved in this. She doesn't deserve to witness any more of this madness."

"Dude, I am not going to tell her what to do. She looks like she slaps really hard."

"That she does," I say, "that she does . . . "

Twenty minutes pass, and I'm beginning to think we're lost, then she flicks her lighter and holds the flame over her head, revealing a handle sticking out of the ceiling. "This door will lead you into the laundry room. Once you go up there, you are on your own."

"Okay."

Mercedes hands me a small remote. I stuff it in my pocket without thinking.

"There's a button on that," she says. "Once you're sure you've gained the guards' attention, hit it. It'll trigger an alarm that I have on my person and we will come barging in. We'll already be waiting at the mono station—hopefully. Just make sure to give us enough time to get there. An hour should cover it, I think. Any questions?"

"Yes," I say, "where the hell do you have the alarm? You have no clothes on."

"You probably don't want to know the answer to that," Mercedes says.

"Gross."

"Incredibly."

"Just make sure that Molly doesn't come," I tell her. "And whatever happens, whether I make it or not, you get my daughter out of this place. I don't care what you have to do. She must be safe."

Mercedes places her hand on my shoulder. "The first step is yours, Detective."

"Thanks," I say, looking back up at the trap door. Fear has frozen my body. "If I don't make it, you'll get Molly and Ezzy out of the city, right? You'll make sure they are okay."

"Assuming I survive the night," Mercedes says, "you

have my word. Your other friend, the pseudo-Brit, however, is on his own."

"Yeah, that's fine."

"He's kind of an asshole," she says.

I inhale deeply and exhale a hurricane of air. My hand wraps around the trapdoor handle without me even realizing it.

I pull it open. Bright light penetrates my eyeballs.

I climb up into the opening with no idea of what's waiting for me. Indigo himself could be standing up there with a gun pointed at my face, ready to pull the trigger. Anything is possible.

Fuck it.

chapter twenty-two

It takes a moment for my eyes to adjust to the sudden light. My eyes blink through the blurriness until an image forms in front of me: a man wearing a white apron.

"Excuse me," he says, "but who the fuck are you?"

"Umm," I say, and drive a right hook across his jaw. He collapses to the linoleum, out cold. Still, though, there's no telling how long he'll be out, so I grab him by the shoulders and drag him to the trapdoor, letting his dead bodyweight drop hard into the tunnel.

Washers and driers are spread out against the walls, each of them currently active. Thank god there had only been the one guy in here. After that last punch, my fist is throbbing.

"Hey, who the hell are you?" a voice says from behind me. Crap.

I spin around to spot another man in a white apron. This one's holding a laundry basket, which he promptly drops to his feet. I reach in my jacket and pull out my machinegun, pointing it straight at him.

"Not a word!" I shout, and gesture to the opened trapdoor. "Get in."

"Wh-what?"

"Get in the hole! Now!"

The man peeks in the hole, then looks back at me strangely. "Why?"

"Because otherwise I will shoot you in the face. With bullets."

I guess it's a good enough reason. He sits down and scoots off the edge of the hole, dropping down into the tunnel. "Okay," he says, "now what?"

"Just start walking. Eventually, you'll come across a redheaded girl named Molly. Tell her I said hi."

"What?"

I lean over one of the nearby washing machines, unplug it, and tilt it over onto the hole. It is just big enough to cover the whole thing without falling through.

I can still hear the man shouting underneath it, but much more muffled now. It'll have to do.

I return the machinegun back to my jacket pocket. I wonder how long it'll be before I have to take it out again.

I push through the doors of the laundry room and find myself in an empty hallway. So far, so good. Sneaking down the hallway, I turn into yet another hallway. I repeat this action three more times before finding another door that leads into a wide, expansive room occupied by the population of a small town. The chatter of hundreds of people hits me all at once, and I have to take a moment to recover.

I press against a wall, behind a few tables where people are dining over beer and meat. The room is vast, bigger than I could have ever imagined. People crowd around slot machines and craps tables. Their expressions show horror and disgust, yet they're so emotionally involved, they can't leave.

A woman steps in front of me. She is all skin except for her three-inch long skirt and bra. She practically shoves her tits in my face, blocking my path.

"Hey there, stranger," she says.

"Uh, hi," I say to her breasts.

"You lookin' for some company?" she asks.

"Excuse me?"

"You want your dick sucked, mister? Your butthole plugged, perhaps? Your nipples tattooed?"

"Um . . . not presently." I step around her. I quickly

head toward the crowd of people circling around a large steel cage in the center of the room.

The prostitute shouts, "Have it your way, creep!"

I push myself into the crowd, not stopping until I'm almost against the cage wall. Inside the ring, two scraggly men fight for their lives. Both are covered in blood. Their ribs are bruised and beaten. Discarded teeth litter the floor. They have no weapons, only their fists.

I am able to watch for a moment, and then I have to look away. Everyone else is cheering, pleading for more bloodshed. This is entertainment. This is what makes their adrenalin run, this is what makes them hard.

"Yeaaah, bash his fucking skull in!" shouts a young kid standing next to me, and my jaw drops.

"Aerosol!"

The kid stops, looks at me quizzically. "Dickhead, that you?"

"Yeah."

"You remember your real name yet?"

I nod at him. "It was Dickhead after all."

"Wow, I'm a good guesser," he says, and returns his attention back to the bloodbath in the cage before us.

This is sick. Vile. I try to push myself away from the cage, but run face-first into a huge biker's chest, bouncing off him like he's a brick wall. He looks down at me with his scruffy biker beard, eyeing me up and down.

"Fuck's the matter with you?" he says.

"This is disgusting, you all should be ashamed of yourself."

"You ain't from around here, are you?" he asks, placing his paw of a hand on my shoulder, squeezing it tightly.

My reflexes respond instantly, and my knee drives up into the man's crotch, sending him to the floor. Fortunately, the bloodbath occurring in the cage is enough of a distraction for the rest of the casino's patrons to not notice my lashing out. I quickly jump over the fallen man and head back out of the crowd, bumping into the prostitute I'd previously ignored.

She gives me a mean look and goes, "Oh, if it ain't the creep."

Off in the distance I hear, "Larry, what the fuck you doin' on the floor, man?"

"Some jackass hit me in the balls!" the biker yells from the crowd. "I'm gonna kill him!"

I offer a pathetic smile at the prostitute. "You know what, why don't we go someplace privately so I can prove exactly what I am?"

"Hmmph," the prostitute says. "Suppose you don't have any cash?"

I pull out the $2000 casino chip I'd taken from the trench coat back at the river. The prostitute's eyes brighten like she's just seen the face of god.

"Mister, follow me." She grabs my crotch and leads me away from the bar, through a few crowded lobbies and hallways, up an elevator, up a set of stairs, and through a door marked ROOM C. The room itself is quite small, just big enough for a bed, and not a nice bed at that. Just a dirty old mattress on the floor, and against the wall there's a toilet. A sink is built in next to it, with a mirror above it.

The woman locks the door behind us, smiling big and stupidly. "Can I see that chip again, please?"

I hand it to her. I have no need for it, after all. I never plan to spend a dime in this miserable place.

She holds it up close to her eyes, rubbing its texture. "Wow, this sure is something."

"What's your name?" I ask her.

"Mister, for this kind of dough, you can call me your personal wet dream."

"Okay, whatever," I say. "Look, I don't really want to do anything."

"Nonsense!" Wet Dream laughs, and pushes me on the bed. "I am going to give you the best time of your life. Trust me, honey, I'll be worth every penny . . . "

She takes her bra off, letting her tits drop down a few inches over her flat stomach. Before I can immediately respond, she leaps on my lap, pushing her chest in my face. One of her nipples gets sucked into my mouth, and for a moment I can't breathe.

Wet Dream thrusts her breast harder into my face, and I'm squirming underneath her, trapped. In an attempt to get her off of me, I reach around to grab her, but only end up squeezing her amazingly crafted ass. Jesus Christ, now I have an erection. This isn't good, this isn't good at all.

"Oh, what ever do we have here?" Wet Dream says, reaching down and rubbing her palm against my spitefully increasing hard-on.

"No, please, stop," I try to say, but her goddamn breast muffles my voice.

She begins unzipping my jeans, reaching her hand inside and grabbing a hold of my cock, and I know I can't let this continue, I really can't, except okay, maybe just a little longer, Jesus, just a little longer—

No!

Regretting it immediately, I swing my fist around and punch the woman in the side of the face, sending her flying off my lap and against the hardwood floor. I sit on the bed for a moment, completely frozen in shock, my cock still sticking out of my zipper.

Wet Dream lies on the floor for a moment, rubbing her red cheek, and smiles. "Baby, I didn't know you liked to play like that. Oh, honey, we are going to have some fun."

"What? No . . . "

"You want to hit me, baby?" She stands up on her knees, lowering her head down on my lap. "I'll let you in on a little secret . . . pain makes me orgasm, like, *so hard*. Hit me baby. Make me come."

Her tongue slides out of her mouth and attempts to make contact with my stupid penis, but I push her away. This time I zip back up.

"No," I say, "this isn't what I want."

"Well, what do you want then, baby?" she asks. "Do you want a whip? I have a whip. I have *tons* of whips, oh my god, you don't even know."

"No! Dammit! I don't want any whips. I want information."

She pauses, eyebrow raised. "Information?"

"Yes."

Wet Dream thinks for a moment, then smiles naughtily. "Oh, I see."

I sigh. "I doubt it."

"You want to know about the other johns. What we do. Like, what's the craziest thing I've ever done."

I shake my head, annoyed. "I would rather hear about your boss. Indigo."

Wet Dream's smile dies instantly. "I am not going to tell you about what I do with him. That's private business. Besides, he'd kill me if I talked about what he was like in bed. So, you're just going to have to want something else, I don't care how much money you offer me."

"I don't care what you guys do together. I want to know about where he is right now. I have some personal business to settle with him."

Wet Dream looks at me, confused.

"So," I say, "are you going to help me find him or what?"

"Um . . . " She scrambles up to her feet, shouting, "Help! Guards! Help! Help!"

"Hey lady, what the hell?" I jump up off the mattress and run over to the door, grabbing a hold of Wet Dream before she can unlock the door. She lets out a loud screech and scratches her nails across my face.

"*Get off of me!*" she screams. "*Help! Somebody help!*"

"Stop screaming!"

"Help!"

She lashes her hand out at me again, but this time I catch it in mid-strike. "Look," I say, and bash my forehead into her face. She drops to the floor, limp.

"I'm sorry."

I drag her body over to the mattress and flop her down on her stomach. Who knows how long she'll be out. I hope I didn't kill her.

Well, at least she's led me away from the crowded areas of the casino. Now I'll have some quiet alone time to explore this godforsaken place in peace. I unlock the door and quietly slip out into the hallway. There are multiple doors lined up down the hall, each one marked with a different letter.

I walk down and randomly open a door marked ROOM G. Inside, I discover a naked man tied up against the wall, limbs spread to their fullest extent. A woman wearing black leather holds a blowtorch up to his scrotum. The man immediately begins screaming through his gag ball, and the woman gives me a mean look.

"Wait your turn!"

I close the door and continue exploring the hallway, vowing not to open another door with a letter marked on it.

This casino is too big, it's going to take me forever to find what I want. I'll be wandering these hallways until I'm dead of old age, if I'm not too careful. It's one after another. All of them housing random, ominous doors that I really don't care to go through. Ezzy isn't going to be in any of these rooms. Indigo is going to have her someplace safe, someplace a person won't just stumble upon accidentally.

I find it startling that I don't run into any casino employees. It seems to me they'd at least be passing through every once in a while, but no, the hallways remain empty save for my own presence.

After a while, just when dementia has begun to fully grow on me, I discover an elevator. There's only one way to go: UP.

I press the button and inhale dreadfully as the door closes. The machinegun in my pocket feels heavy and hazardous as the elevator carries me up to my inevitable doom.

Then the elevator stops, and the doors slide open. I walk into a wall of darkness. I can tell by the way my footsteps echo that the room I'm in is large and epic, yet all I can see is black.

That is, except for the lighted object up ahead—the white sun in the center of a galaxy of darkness.

There's no mistaking the object.

It's a baby's crib.

And coming from the crib is a baby's cry.

chapter twenty-three

Ezzy.

My baby girl.

My legs take off at once, guiding me through the darkness and toward the light. Ezzy's in the crib. She's really there. For a moment I had feared all I'd find would be a voice recorder. But no. Here she is, wrapped up in a blanket. Her crying ceases as soon as she sees me, and her sad face reforms into a smile of joy.

"Da-doo!" she exclaims, reaching her arms up to hold me.

I reach down to grab her, but freeze when the darkness in the room is replaced with a menacing brightness.

Of course it's too good to be true.

I jump up, leaving Ezzy in the crib—still safe—and spin around. Ten feet from me stands an extremely tall and lanky man. He studies me with cataract-glazed eyes.

"Indigo," I whisper.

"Detective Oasis," Indigo whispers back.

Behind him are about a dozen pale doctors. Harvies.

They stand between us and the door.

Gritting my teeth, I say, "This is going to end with me walking through that door, so you best get out of my way while I'm still giving you the chance."

Indigo laughs, but it doesn't sound genuine. More like a broken machine on its last few minutes of life.

"You have no idea how this ends," he says. It comes out almost like a snake's slither.

"You may have everyone else conned, you bastard," I say, "but I'm not one of your blind followers. Stand aside or I'll . . . "

"You'll what?" he asks, amused.

"I'll fuck your shit up, is what I'll do."

It's not the best threat, but I'm not a hero in an action movie. I'm just a confused lunatic trying to save his daughter.

"Oh, poor you, haven't you realized reality is a mirage? Don't you understand what's happening, Detective Oasis? Your mind's playing tricks on you."

"You tried to kill me."

Indigo shakes his head. "No," he says, "I tried to improve you. Before, you were faulty. You were a sneak. A liar. I tried to make you perfect. And I failed. I do not fail often."

He hasn't blinked once, the whole time he's been looking at me. I wonder if he's ever blinked once in his life. Evil like him, maybe it doesn't have to.

"Save the shit," I say. "Improve me? You're a goddamn hack and you know it."

He raises his eyebrow at me this time. "Take a look around you, Oasis. My harvies are real. You are being ridiculous."

As if on cue, the harvies begin to flicker in and out of existence like dying light bulbs. Who knows who they had once been?

"Of course they're real, you tyrant. It's a shame you can't see how much they despise you, too—how, deep down, they wish to kill you."

"Some do," Indigo says. "They are disposed of."

"Like me."

Indigo nods approvingly. "Like you."

"I came back."

"I'll fix it."

I spit on the ground and start pacing back and forth, creating a protective wall in front of Ezzy and the crib. My hand casually slides into my jean pocket and my finger presses down on the remote button Mercedes had given me. I don't know if I've succeeded in distracting any guards, but I know I might not have another chance to trigger it.

"Admit why you're really doing all this," I say. "Tell me you're doing it all for the money. I want to hear it from your own mouth."

"But, Detective Oasis," Indigo says, "you are mistaken. As you should very well know, this is all for our beloved Conundrae. He is our true Lord and Master. Soon He will rise, and we will be His family. Everyone else will be food. Don't mock me, Oasis. I've killed you once. I'll do it again."

I burst out laughing. I can't help it. "You actually believe this. The whole time coming here, I was thinking I was about to go up against a criminal mastermind. Instead, you're just batshit crazy. You're a psycho and nothing more."

Indigo frowns. It's the first sincere expression. "It's a shame, really, that you won't be alive when Conundrae does rise. It'd be orgasmic just to see your face when you realize how wrong you are. But you'll be gone long before then, you and your cunt of a child."

He hits a cord and he knows it. We remain standing, eyes burning, preparing to engage in battle.

A voice speaks up from Indigo's waist: a small, black walkie-talkie.

"Uh, boss? You're not going to believe this, but we're under attack. A bunch of, uh, naked people running around here with weapons. They're killing everyone. Holy shit, what do we do? What do we—*ARRGGHHHH*—"

Indigo fumbles for the walkie-talkie clipped to his waist, and in his panic, drops it to the floor, at his feet. In the time it takes him to bend down, pick it up, and stand, I've already pulled the machinegun from my jacket and trained the sights on him.

His eyes widen. Caught.

His surprise quickly fades. A smile returns to his pale face.

"The thing is," I say, "it doesn't matter if I can't remember who I really am, or if you've made up some false god to get rich. In the end, it's all artificial—memory, money, gods, and identities. None of it matters. The only thing that anyone should ever give a shit about is the *now*. And right now, all your men are dying, and you are alone. Right now, I am going to take my little girl, and we are going to be safe. Because right now, you've lost, and I've won."

The smile on Indigo's face transgresses into full on laughter. *Crackles.*

"Oh, you are *precious*," he says.

It doesn't matter.

I squeeze the trigger and I don't let go until bullets stop spitting out of the muzzle and melting into his flesh. He flies a few feet back and lands flat on his back. Blood and smoke pour from his body like the cauldron of a cannibal.

And my ears are ringing, but it doesn't prevent me from hearing every one of the harvies in the room screech like mad banshees. They explode simultaneously, leaving behind in their dust nothing more than small, confused spiders. They flee into the shadows.

"Well, that was easy."

Ezzy's cries also overpower the ringing in my ears. I drop the empty machinegun and pick her up, hugging her close to my chest. I try not to wonder what kind of damage I may have just wreaked upon her own ears.

"Oh, baby, it's okay, Daddy is here. It's all right now. I promise."

chapter twenty-four

But she keeps crying. We need to get out of here.

It doesn't take as long to get back to the casino's main floor as it had taken getting up to Indigo's private penthouse. Now I know my way around. We take the elevator down and quickly move through the labyrinth of hallways. I hold Ezzy close to me, hoping she stops crying, but of course she doesn't. Gunshots are going off like fireworks. Thankfully we don't encounter any trouble in the hallways.

Downstairs, that's where the real action is. In the main casino room—the location of the fighting cage and the slots—the world is a bloodbath. Corpses litter the floor like cigarette butts on the street—both casino henchmen and naked Refragatio alike. It's not just them but the patrons, too. Everybody. Covered in bullet holes. Covered in arrows. Covered in death. Jesus.

But they're not all dead. The battle rages on right before our eyes. A man in a suit hides behind a pushed-over bar table, hands trembling as he holds his pistol up to defend himself from any attacks. But he's too slow: one of the Refragatio comes running and flips over the table, decapitating the man with a machete in mid-motion. His head goes rolling across the room like a loose marble.

The machete-wielding Refragatio is shot down by another guard seconds later, who in turn is shot through the eye by an arrow.

Ezzy continues to cry.

We hide behind the bar, crouching under the drink counter. I try to muffle her sobs by pushing her face against my chest, although I don't know why I'm even bothering, given the volume of the gunfire.

A few people scream from another room. The sound alone makes my skin turn cold. This is a disaster. I made this happen. What else did I expect?

Ezzy drools down my chest, and I think, at least she's safe. That's what this is all about. I've saved her. I've taken down Indigo. We are going to be safe.

Footsteps approach the bar. They stop next to where we're hiding. The intruder's breaths are heavy.

We sit there for a moment, Ezzy and I behind the counter, holding our breaths, the assailant two feet away. Both of us are waiting for the other to move. If I don't do anything, then it'll give the other person the upper hand. Best to act now while they're not expecting me to actually act. There's an empty beer bottle on the floor next to us. Sighing, I grab it by the neck and jump up, holding the bottle back over my head with full intentions of bashing it in the face of whoever is standing here.

"Whoa, stop!" Molly shouts, raising her arms up in defense.

I manage to stop just before engaging into full-on swing-action. "What the hell are you doing here?" I ask, dropping the beer bottle.

"Mommy!" Ezzy exclaims from in my arms, reaching out for Molly.

Molly brightens. "Oh, god, *Ezzy!*"

The baby practically leaps from my arms to hers. It's like I don't even exist. I can't help but smile. Molly pushes Ezzy's face into her chest.

Molly peeps an eye over Ezzy's head. "You did it," she says.

I give her a knowing nod, wanting to hug her like she's hugging our daughter, but still alert enough to know that we're nowhere close to being in the clear yet. The sounds of people screaming and gunshots going off penetrate the casino's interior like thunder in a titanium barrel.

"I told Mercedes not to let you come. What are you doing here?"

"What do you think?" Molly says. "I came for our baby girl, the same reason you're here."

"Then why the bloody hell am I here?" the Rev asks, and it's the first time I notice he's standing behind her, rubbing his ass. "I don't got no fookin' tyke."

"Because you were scared to be left alone in the big old scary tunnels," Molly says without bothering to look back.

"Ha!" the Rev says, cheeks turning red. "That's . . . that's a good one, there, Mol."

"Bobby," Molly says, more serious now. "Did you get him? Indigo—did you kill him?"

"He's gone," I tell her. "It's all right now. But we still need to get out of here, fast. Where's Mercedes?"

"Beats the hell outta me," the Rev says.

Molly doesn't know, either. "She ran in right ahead of us, and we lost her almost immediately. She could be dead for all I know. God knows almost everyone else is."

There's another gunshot from a nearby room, and someone screams.

"Not everyone," the Rev says.

I shake my head, wanting to be done with this nonsense already. "Screw it, let's just go. We can meet her at the mono."

"Sounds like a plan, mate," the Rev says. I crawl over the bar counter and we head out of the cage room, making sure to grab a discarded pistol along the way.

The front entrance is in our sights. Our speed increases, and it feels like everything actually is going to be okay. What we'll do once we make it out of the casino, I have no idea. I don't care about that right now. All I'm concerned about is getting *out* of here. We'll figure the rest out later.

"Oasis," a voice says, and we stop dead in our tracks.

Mercedes comes stumbling through the entrance lobby, falling to the ground in front of us. She scrambles back to her feet, leaving behind bloody handprints on the marble floor as she gets up.

"Oh, Christ," I whisper, helping her regain her balance. "They got you."

Mercedes gasps for breath, struggling to form coherent words. She falls down again and grabs onto the Rev's leg to keep herself from hitting the ground. She reaches inside his pants, and the Rev goes wide-eyed. "Oy, the hell is this?"

She removes her hand and stands up again, ignoring the Rev. "Indigo," she says to me. "We were winning, we had taken over . . . then Indigo came. Killed us, killed us all."

"That's impossible," I say. "I shot Indigo. I made sure he was dead."

Mercedes looks at me with absolute dread. "Something's happened. He isn't normal. He's changed."

"What do you mean?"

"I don't . . . I can't . . . "

"What do we do?"

"If he lives, then the rest of us will die," Mercedes says. "You must stop him. Otherwise . . . nothing has been resolved. All these deaths tonight would have been a waste."

The Rev gives a nervous laugh. "Lass, no offense, but we need to get our sorry arses out of here before we, well, before we end up like you."

"He's right," Molly says, nudging me. "We gotta go, Bobby, *now.*"

Mercedes slips something into my hand, something hard and oval-shaped, something she'd pulled from the Rev's pants, and she goes weak in my arms. She lets out a long, disgusting groan. "Make it mean something, make it *mean something.*"

Then her eyes roll in the back of her head and she says no more.

I gently lower her limp body to the floor. I slip the object Mercedes handed me into my pocket, not looking at it but knowing what it is all the same. Molly grabs onto my jacket collar, trying to drag me out the door with her. Ezzy is saying, "Da-doo, get up, Da-doo, get up!"

"Come on, Bob-O," the Rev says. "She's gone, let her be, we gotta jet."

"Let's *go*," Molly says.

"No," I mutter, already regretting what I'm saying. "She's right."

"*What?*" Molly says.

"Everyone here died tonight, everyone who helped us. They all died. For what?"

"For helping us save the life of our daughter, dammit," Molly says. "Now come *on*."

I stand up, finding it hard to take my eyes off Mercedes. Because she's right. If we leave now, with Indigo still alive, then what was the point of any of it? Yeah, we saved Ezzy, but for how long? Indigo will keep looking for us, and he *will* find us eventually. As long as Indigo is alive, we will never be safe.

"Listen," I say, turning back to Molly, trying not to let my voice crack. "This isn't done. I haven't finished what I started. You guys, you need to go ahead without me. Get on the mono, retreat back to the tunnels with the rest of the Refragatio. I'll meet up with you guys later, after I've taken care of this. If I don't come back by sunrise, well . . . get the hell out of the city, as fast as you can."

"Are you fucking nuts?" Molly says, crying. "You aren't staying behind. We need to go. *You* need to be with us."

"I will," I tell her, "I'll make it back in time. I promise, sweetheart, nothing bad will happen." I kiss her on the lips, tasting the bitter salt in her tears.

"I get no say in this, do I?" she says, and I shake my

head and as I kiss her again, Ezzy wraps her arms around my neck and hugs me.

I tell myself that she'll be hugging me again soon. I don't know if that's true. I want Molly to believe it is, though. *I* want to believe it is.

"Just go," I tell her, "and imagine I'm right behind you. I'm off to save the world again."

Molly opens her mouth to say something, then she closes it, thinks for a moment, and finally says, "I love you, Bobby."

"I love you, too," I tell her, and then both her and Ezzy are running out the door, Ezzy shouting my name (*"Da-doo, Da-doo"*) as they leave.

The Rev pauses before moving. He looks over his shoulder at me like he's expecting never to talk to me again. He says, "Vivian."

"Excuse me?"

He clears his throat. "My name, my real name. It's Vivian."

I can't help it. I laugh.

"You royal cunt," he says.

"Love you too, Rev," I say, and watch as he limps out the casino entrance.

I make sure the pistol in my hands is loaded, and I turn back around, heading for where Mercedes had come from. I follow the sound of bullets. The sound of screams.

I arrive at the bottom of a stairway. The steps are covered in random limbs and thick puddles of gore. Indigo stands at the top of the steps, slowly walking down toward me. He wields a huge shotgun, blowing away the last few survivors unlucky enough to be in his way.

Indigo's mouth curls into a snarl that makes my heart skip a beat. His face is deformed and dripping of melted flesh, thanks to my previous machinegun escapades. Yet it doesn't seem to stop him. If anything, he's stronger—faster.

How is he still walking?

How is he still *breathing?*

217

Indigo keeps his eyes on me as he walks down the steps, even as he pulls the trigger of his shotgun and blows away the already dying corpses crawling at his feet. He smiles at me, enjoying this. He's looking at me like he's saying, *I told you this would happen, you didn't believe me, but now you know.*

And he's right. Now I know.

Fuck.

Now he's at the end of the steps, and he's right in front of me. Our eyes become one.

I say, "You were dead."

And he says, "So were you."

I forget about keeping my heart intact and focus every single cell in my body on making Indigo a whole lot uglier. It doesn't even fucking faze him.

He lifts the shotgun. I lift my pistol. He's faster.

A noise erupts my eardrums and I'm flat on my back, bleeding out of my stomach. My vision dies and I'm back home in the warmth of darkness.

All I hear is Indigo laughing.

chapter twenty-five

Darkness. And then light.

A light so bright and sharp I can feel it stab into my eyeballs. It pains my teeth. My jaw unhinges and a scream attempts to escape, but my throat is too weak, and only a low pathetic squeal is audible.

The light, it's from a flashlight. It's hooked up to some mechanism above the seat that has become my new prison. It's like a gurney, keeping me in a slanted vertical position. Metal straps pin me to the cushion.

I can't move. I can't think. I can't breathe.

A numbness overwhelms my stomach, makes my body warm, my mind dizzy.

Oh fuck, *what is this?*

The brightness of the light slowly begins to fade, and Indigo's face becomes more apparent, hovering above me with the same malformed snarl.

"Welcome back," he whispers.

"Where the fuck am I?"

He chuckles. The sound makes me want to vomit my soul away.

"You're back home, Detective Oasis," he says. "Where you always belonged."

"Where's Molly—where's Ezzy?"

"Don't really care about them at the moment," he says. "I'll find them later, when I'm bored and hungry. Right now, you're the center of attention. You're the premium meat."

"What the hell does that even mean?" I try to move, but there's no struggle, it's impossible.

"It means," Indigo says, "that I've taken quite a liking to you. I tried to turn you already, and it didn't work. You kept fighting. The spider, the parasite left your body. That never happens."

I'm lucky to wiggle my nose to blink my eyes, lucky to open my mouth as I scream.

"Your mind," Indigo says, "it's unlike any I have ever encountered. It devoured my spider, my little harvester converter, and spat it right out. I don't know what makes you so special, Detective Oasis, but I know it'd be a shame to let you go to waste."

This is fucked. This is so fucked.

"You told me that you didn't believe in Conundrae. You called me a fake, a con artist," Indigo says. "What you don't remember is, that's exactly what you said last time you were in this chair. Last time, though, your words angered me. All those years you spent supporting our Master, and it was all fraudulent. I became very, very upset."

I'm thinking about Molly, about Ezzy, about the Rev and everyone else I no longer remember. My father, my mother. My dead brother.

Where are they now?

"But this time," Indigo says, "I am not so mad. I am more . . . amused. I am sure you're wondering why I am still standing. I should be dead. Well, Detective Oasis, the truth is, I've been dead for a while now. The truth is, it's not just you and I that's in this room right now. It's not just me that's talking to you."

Fuck, fuck this is crazy, this is fucking crazy . . .

Indigo's cold, cataract eyes transform from a state of listlessness into a set of mesmerizing purple flames.

He stares into my soul and I feel it melting away.

"This world is mine, Detective Oasis," Indigo says, only it's not Indigo anymore.

"*Conundrae,*" I whisper.

The demon nods.

"Now that I'm here, I am going to need someone to lead my army of harvies. There's lots of food out there, Oasis, and I am *starving*."

"*No . . .*"

"*Yes* . . . and your mind is just what I need to lead them. It's been a long time coming, Detective, but we've finally made it. What have I always said?" He snarls. "Slowly but surely, sugar pie. Slowly but surely."

Something tickles my skin. It only takes me a moment to realize it's a spider crawling on my neck. Not just one spider, but *dozens*.

"*NOOOO!*" I scream, my fingers straining to stretch inside my jacket pocket. They just reach, curling around the object Mercedes gave me during her final moments.

"Shh," says Conundrae, "it'll be over soon. And then . . . we feast."

Molly, her face, her long red hair. The way I first saw her when I walked into the bar, the way she danced, and the way her beautiful eyes brightened when they found me. I want to be back in bed with her, at our shitty little apartment. I want to be holding her. I want to be kissing her. I want to feel her skin, oh god, I want to feel her breath. I want to place my lips on her chest and kiss her heartbeats.

The spiders enter my flesh and all I can hear is the demon laughing.

Inside my jacket pocket, I'm finally able to pull the pin on the grenade, and then I'm the one laughing.

The darkness is overcome by the brightness of Molly's smile burnt into my memory.

She's holding Ezzy, and we're all together again.

Forever.

about the author

Max Booth III is a novelist, screenwriter, editor, podcaster, and publisher. He is the author of *Abnormal Statistics, Maggots Screaming!, Touch the Night*, and many other titles too spooky to name here. His film, *We Need to Do Something*, was released by IFC Midnight in 2021. With his wife, Lori, he co-runs Ghoulish Books, a small press and indie bookstore based in San Antonio, Texas. Learn more about him at TalesFromTheBooth.com.

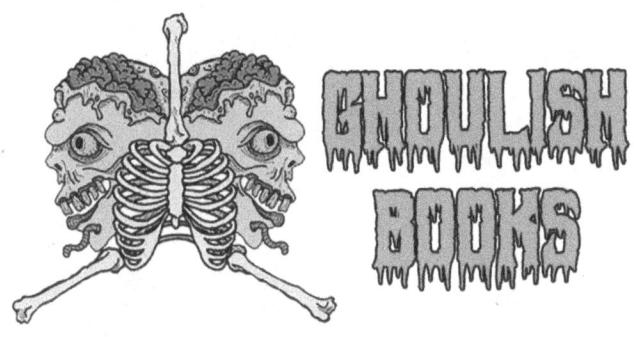

Patreon:
www.patreon.com/ghoulishbooks

Website:
www.Ghoulish.rip

Facebook:
www.facebook.com/GhoulishBooks

Twitter:
@GhoulishBooks

Instagram:
@GhoulishBookstore

Linktree:
linktr.ee/ghoulishbooks